I0679425

DRAGONFLY

This is a work of fiction. The events described are imaginary. Real places are used fictitiously. Any resemblance of characters and events to real life is coincidental.

Dragonfly
(Meadowlark Book 2)
Copyright © 2021 by Julie Embers
All rights reserved.
Published by Red Pill Hippie in Eugene, Oregon.

No part of this book may be reproduced, distributed, or transmitted in any form or by any means, or stored in a database or retrieval system, without the written permission of the author except in the case of brief quotations embodied in critical articles and reviews.

Second Paperback Edition.
ISBN: 978-0-9962795-6-7
Library of Congress: 2021918963

Printed in the United States of America.

Cover photographs: Arman Zhenikeyev, Zumphoto. Title page image: *Paul Wilson.* Backcover image: *LHG.* Flower image: *Olya Creative Art.* Biohazard image: *Blumer1979.* Fonts: Caribbean's Treasure; Northwood High. Logo: *Alexkava.*

FOR **DAN**

DRAGONFLY

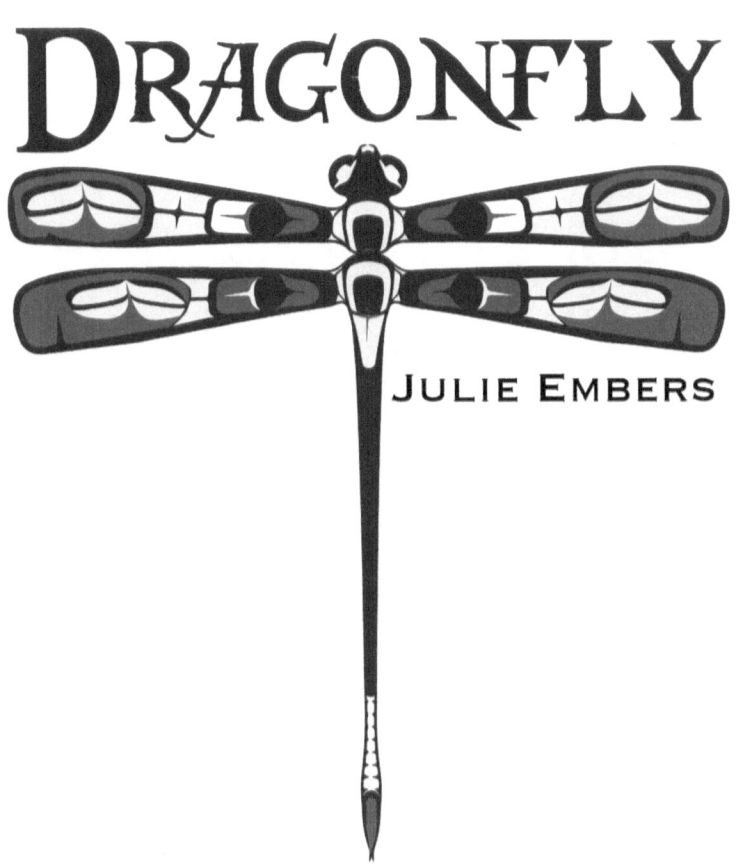

JULIE EMBERS

MEADOWLARK BOOK TWO

Insignia

Rain patters on the roof, blanketing the trailer park.

Today's the day, thinks Anna. She rolls over. The smell of beer wafts into her nostrils. Her mother snuck into her bed last night and passed out, just like every night since Anna can remember.

Her mother's skin has lost its elasticity from decades of cigarette smoke, and she reeks of it. What life the worn woman has left drips out every day, slowly running dry. Anna tried to stop it, but poverty will kill her mother, just as it will Anna.

She tucks a greasy lock of hair behind her mother's ear.

The folds of Mom's forehead deepen. Her eyes open and she whispers, "Good luck today."

Easy for her to say. She isn't the one getting a scope shoved up her ass. *I can't believe I've gotta work today.*

The floor heater kicks on. The pink feathers of a dreamcatcher, hung beside the window, brush the aqua-painted wall. Mom bought it when she found out she was pregnant with Anna. It was supposed to catch nightmares, but that isn't enough when your whole life is one. The window sits high upon the wall, hard to see out of unless you're standing on the bed.

The clock Anna scored at a junk store last week still works. Its red-glowing digits shift into another minute. *Time to go.* She slides out of bed, pulls on a worn pair of Converse sneakers and makes for the kitchen. A four-liter jug of colon cleanse sits on the counter, waiting for her. She grabs it, accepting its burden, and heads out the door. The city bus stop is right up the hill, out of sight. The driver won't wait, not even a second, if she is late. She shoots through a mud puddle, splashing the water enough that it soaks her fishnets and seeps through her sneakers.

The bus stop comes into view. Red brake lights cut through the grey tapestry and sink away, toward town. She has missed the bus.

"Shit." She slides the jug onto the bench, catching a breath. She won't have enough time to drink the stuff before the café opens.

Old Ms. Murphy sits beneath the bus stop awning, hunched like a corpse. Her eyes roll in Anna's direction and down at the jug.

"Was that the seven o'clock?" Anna asks.

Dark-grey smoke spits from the bus's exhaust as it speeds up over the bridge in the distance.

Ms. Murphy digs into her purse, pulls out a piece of butterscotch candy, and offers it to Anna. Its yellow-plastic wrapper adds a splash of color to the otherwise grey world.

Anna takes it to be polite, but slides it into the pocket of her skirt. She never cared much for candy. Her father thought loading her up on sugar would wipe away the days he was never there.

"Thanks," Anna says.

Mrs. Murphy brushes a thick silver curl from her cheek and pops a candy, sucking it hard.

Has her hair always been so kinky? Anna wonders. Her husband, Frank, went bald years ago. Anna looks down at the jug of cleanse. Rumors were it was prostate cancer that did him in.

Raindrops slide down the plastic container.

Anna knows it wasn't his prostate. She saw him with the same jug, waiting at the same stop, for the same fate. It was colon cancer. She would put money on it. She glances at Ms. Murphy, wondering if it was hard getting up everyday and getting dressed. How many times has she accidentally cooked for two? How long are the days when you're alone? "I'm sorry about Frank."

The old woman forces a smile and nods in appreciation.

"Your pumpkins look beautiful." Anna glances back toward the cul-de-sac. Their trailer park houses aren't visible from the bus stop, but there are two raised-bed garden boxes in her side yard. In the summer they burst with life. Now, long green vines stretch into the neighbor's yard, dragging pumpkins. Anna turns back around, bumping her fingers against the jug.

When Anna was little, Frank used to water those boxes for an hour—down to the second. He caught her watching him one day and called her over. "You ever have a tomato fresh out of the ground?" he asked.

She shook her head. "Mom buys the canned ones."

A grin swept across his lips. His eyes brightened. He bent down, saying, "Pick one. Whichever one you want."

There were small ones: yellow, green, orange. Deep in the middle of the vines was a big fat crimson one, with black bleeding down from the stem. She looked back up at him. He nodded in approval and she reached in.

"Now," he said, "you have to twist it."

Anna stretched her fingers around it, twisting. It popped off the vine and she pulled it out between the leaves. It was bigger than her fist.

"Well, look at that," he said. "It's bigger than your heart." He kneeled. "It's amazing what we find, when we go looking for it."

It wasn't long before the tomatoes were left to rot, as he withered away.

Anna hooks her fingers to the jug's handle, staring at it. "It was colon cancer, wasn't it?" she asks.

Mrs. Murphy rests a hand on Anna's.

"Did it hurt?" Anna says.

Mrs. Murphy squeezes Anna's hand, drawing her eyes away.

"Was he ready to go...?" Anna clenches the jug, not really wanting an answer—the dreaded answer that every single person fears. That she'll die. That she'll never be ready when the abyss of death finally swallows her whole.

Mrs. Murphy's lips press together. The wind picks up. Her silver hair blows like drying laundry. She sucks on the candy, spiraling it around in her mouth.

The next bus pops up over the hill.

"I'm scared of dying," Anna says. "I'm not ready."

Mrs. Murphy squeezes her hand one last time before the bus stops in front of them. Then she lets go.

On the bus Anna takes the back, and Mrs. Murphy sits up front like usual. The ride is always the same. Houses blur into the sharp lines of businesses and traffic lights.

The bus jerks forward, stopping. The doors open and the wind reaches in, dragging Anna out. La Café is still blocks away, but not far enough to make it worth waiting for a connecting route. By now, the café should have opened 10 minutes ago.

Wind pounds against her cheeks. She has no idea how she is going to juggle taking orders and drinking the whole jug of cleanse in two hours.

Rain drains from the sky. Water penetrates her sneakers, soaking her toes. A gust pushes against her, counteracting every step.

The streets are still sleeping. Lampposts cast a yellow glow against the large café window, causing the Eiffel Tower, etched into its glass, to twinkle. She pulls a set of keys from her pocket. Raindrops trickle down her fingers and splatter against the glass door. She turns the knob and a second breeze pushes it open.

The soft bell on the ceiling jingles like crazy.

The thin rubber soles of her sneakers squeak against the floor. Her stomach gurgles as the door closes behind her. The high school campus across the street is quiet. *Thank God*. It is too damn early to deal with the spoiled kids who can afford five-dollar coffees.

She passes the counter and rounds the espresso machine, entering the prep area, where she sets down the jug. On top of the morning routine of starting pastries and coffee machines, she has to down the whole damn thing. *Two fucking hours*. It can't be too bad.

Doctor Mullins said, *"Add all three flavor packets."*

That's stupid. Anna rips open the lime-flavored one and pours it into the jug. *Who would want to mix flavors?*

"Drink it cold," she insisted.

Anna pours a glass and takes a swig. It's horrible. It tastes like chemicals, like some kind of bathroom cleaner. She retches, clenching her teeth to force it back down, slamming the cup onto the counter. *Two fucking hours. There's no way I'll finish the whole thing.* But if she doesn't, she will have to reschedule the colonoscopy. She will have to repeat all the fasting she did. Her fingers shake as she tears open the other two flavor packets, dumping them in.

The café bell jingles.

Great. She lets out a grunt and shoves the jug into the freezer. It is too early for customers.

An old man waits at the counter. Three turquoise beads secure an eagle's feather to his grey hair below his right ear.

"Good morning," Anna says, clearing her throat, reminding herself that her problems aren't his. "What would you like?"

"More time," he says. A smile stretches across his clay-colored cheeks. "And a green tea."

She nods and jots it on an order slip. "I'll bring it right out."

He looks around the place and takes the closest booth to the counter—the booth with a mosaic dragonfly in-place of a window.

Anna returns to the prep area. It is an easy order that she serves in three minutes. Then she returns to the freezer. Cold air pours out across the floor, taunting her wet shoes. She stares at

7

the jug, takes a long, deep breath, and grabs it. This time she fills the cup halfway and downs it like a shot glass. *Shit, that's nasty.* Her stomach pushes against the fluid. She glances back toward the storefront, covering her mouth like it will help keep the chemicals down. The espresso machine conceals her from view. *Better check on the old man.* Eight o'clock is creeping up and the campus across the street will soon be bustling. She steps out from the back.

He is sitting still, staring at the café door.

The rain outside pelts softly against its glass.

Her sneakers squeak as she approaches him and he turns his attention to meet hers. "Would you like anything else, sir?"

His eyebrows raise a little.

"Other than time, I mean."

He smiles, shaking his head in refusal.

"Take all the time you'd like." If only in that single moment, he got his wish—all the time he needed. Instead, Anna slides his receipt toward him, stealing some of the seconds he has left. The grains of sand blowing away from both their lives—wasted—on a bill for $3.50.

It is a lot to charge for a green tea, but Anna doesn't set the prices. The owner, Ms. Tumult, has to pay for her new Mercedes, so everything on the menu rose 50 cents. Higher prices means fewer tips, but what Anna really wants is those seconds back.

The gentlemen looks up. Time has carved wrinkles into his skin and stolen the color from his hair. He has seen a world

8

without electronics, a time when stories were told around campfires, a time when trees filled the land. He is a man with stories—ancient stories—the kind that were supposed to be buried with his tribe. Death is coming for him, just like it did for Frank. Just like it will for Anna.

"Thank you," rolls off his crinkled lips.

Anna's intestines cramp. One more smile is enough to excuse her. With it, she sprints around the counter for the back bathroom, flings its door open, and slams it shut behind her. Her fingernails dig through her fishnets, scrunching them to her ankles. Sweat beads in her palms as her bowels empty into the porcelain.

The café bell jingles. Either the old man has left, or there is another customer.

Her knees tremble with the strain on her body. Her fingers shake as she tugs on the toilet paper.

The café bell jingles again. *Shit.* There is at least one new customer in the store now.

She cleans up and washes her hands, letting them drip as she hurries back to the front.

"Good morning, beautiful," one of the regulars, named Dominic, smiles from the other side of the counter.

Blood rushes to the tips of Anna's ears. "What would you like?"

"You..." He leans on the counter.

She swallows hard, smiling. *Did he really just say—?*

"You got any of those Brazil beans in?"

Oh, I'm such an idiot. She notices a girl sitting at the front of the café in the only booth that hugs the front window, hogging the sidewalk view. Her hair is twisted into perfect blonde curls. *He's probably with her, for fuck's sake.* She shakes her head, forcing the thoughts out, feeling completely flat-chested in that moment. "No, they haven't come in yet."

"Then I'll take a tall white mocha and a tall macchiato," he says.

"Do you want whipped cream on that?" Anna asks.

"For the macchiato, I'll take whatever you put on it." He bats his eyelashes and turns to the blonde-girl, extending his voice across the café, "Do you want whipped cream on yours?"

"If you can fit it in," she says.

He looks back at Anna, raising his eyebrows. "You think you could fit it in?"

Oh my god. Anna's cheeks catch fire. *Did he seriously say that?* She picks up the whipped cream canister and presses the nozzle, trying to think of something to say.

Cream swooshes and splatters out.

Great. "I'll be right back." Anna hurries to the prep area. Her stomach growls as she pulls a new canister from the refrigerator. She fills their cups enough to leave room for the whipped cream, squeezes plastic lids on top, and grabs a sleeve, sliding it on the macchiato. She stares at the second sleeve, biting her lip. *Should I?* Her heart pounds. Anna is sick of flirting every day, never getting anything—anything real—from it. She grabs a Magic Marker from the counter and scribbles her phone number on the sleeve. Her heart pounds. She rushes back to him, before she can take it back—change it—fold back into the invisible existence she lingers in.

Dominic smiles as Anna rounds the corner. His teeth alone place him far out of her league. They are the evidence of a childhood wasted at the orthodontist, now bleached to a blinding white on a regular basis.

Anna sets the cups down.

His fingers brush hers as he grabs them. And then he is gone, heading back to her.

Anna glances over at the old man. He is gone. Her intestines tighten. She runs to the table, clears his cup, scoops up the receipt and what money was left, and makes it into the back before her intestines explode. Chemicals pour out as she clenches onto the toilet paper roll.

Her phone rings.

She lets go of the roll, wipes the sweat from her palm and pushes the loose strands of hair from her face. *I couldn't even manage to drink a fucking jug of this shit.* She had wasted all those seconds on a dude who will never call—never think she is anything more than fucking trailer-park trash.

The ringing stops.

She grabs a wad of toilet paper, crumbling it in her hand.

The phone rings again.

She drops the paper in her stockings and pulls the phone from her pocket.

Restricted.

She answers, letting them lead.

"Morning," comes a reverent female voice. "This is Trisha with Corvallis Regional Medical Center. I'm calling to confirm your appointment—"

"I need to reschedule." Pressure builds in her gut. *I can't believe it.* Anna can't even manage to down a jug of chemicals. She will have to start all over again, go through it all over again.

"Uh huh," says the woman, pounding away at her keyboard. "Our next opening is...."

Anna can't hold it. Her intestines let loose, filling the bowl.

The receptionist gives Anna a moment to absorb the burning embarrassment. "How about November twenty-first?"

Right before Thanksgiving? It is the only time Anna ever goes to see her Dad. "You don't have anything else?"

"I have the first two weeks in December...." A deep exhale precedes subtle clicks on the keyboard and mouse.

Anna doesn't say anything. *Why does everything have to be such a—*

"Hold on," she says. The phone clicks and there is silence. It clicks again. "Looks like I just had a cancellation. Lucky for you."

Yeah, *real fucking lucky fir me.*

"How's October thirty-first?"

Halloween? Damn it. Out of all the days. That is even worse than Thanksgiving. Anna forces a, "Yes."

"Eight forty-five," she says.

"In the morning?"

The receptionist doesn't say anything—no doubt struggling with the urge to tell Anna to fuck off, that she shouldn't have canceled. "Yes," she says in a robotic tone, "in the morning."

Anna takes it. At least this way she can still go out and party that night. Either way the results go—she will have a reason to get drunk. She hangs up.

A bead of sweat runs down her temple. She had forgotten about the receipt in her other hand, now clenched in a fist. Ink has smeared into the middle of her palm. A dragonfly with the word "bloodwort" is scribbled on the back of the paper. A $100 bill falls out from beneath it.

INK

ANNA STIFFENS. "DAMN JERRY. YOU DON'T HAVE TO press that hard."

"Just relax," he says. "You're going to screw it up."

She sinks back in the chair and unclenches her fists. Goddamn needles hurt like a mo-fo, but that new ink glistening in her skin, makes the rest of the world dull.

"So did you get your test results?" He leans a little harder, dragging the needle's tip like a razor-blade, slicing through three layers of her skin.

"Jesus, Jerry. You go any deeper ... and I'll bleed out."

He glances up and smiles with crooked, coffee-stained teeth. The caffeine never helps his nerves and his hands shake like a buffer, but his tattoo lines are flawless.

Sweat builds in Anna's palms and she finds her hands clenched into fists again. *Damn, it hurts.* She looks down at the fresh black lines. It is so worth it. Mom will be pissed, though.

The tips of Jerry's rubber gloves smear against her chest. His hair rubs against her chin as he leans closer to her breast.

She sucks a breath through clenched teeth, bearing down on the pain. *Damn.*

"Yeah that area's a bitch. I'm almost done." A few more razor-blade lines run through Anna's skin and then the hum of the machine ceases. Jerry smears the side of his pinky over the thin Twenty-One Pilots shirt covering her breast. "So are you paying for this the old way?"

She pushes him away and grabs a handheld mirror off his station.

He starts to unbuckle his belt.

The curves of ink blend into a rich black dragonfly. A splash of purple makes it look like it's about to flutter off. She slides her fingers along the red, swollen area around it. Its placement is perfectly inline with the curve of her left breast.

Jerry's pants fall to his ankles.

"Chill, Jerry. I have cash this time." She slides off the chair and presses the $100 bill against his chest. The $10 change could have bought her a six-pack of beer, but it is worth leaving to savor the moment.

The neon TATTOO sign in the window buzzes as she steps out onto the sidewalk. It blinks like a bug zapper, sure to draw the nightlife creatures off the sidewalk.

Right about now the pre-Halloween parties will be starting. Three blocks down, music pours out into the street from an aqua-painted door. The bar's front windows capture the sea of people standing elbow-to-elbow, squished inside like sardines, and dressed in costumes. Anna squeezes through a crowd of smokers outside. One beer, just one, before she has to go home and start shitting all over again.

She reaches the aqua door and grabs its worn brass knob. She can always get a beer here. The door is the same color as her bedroom, out of the same can after all; except the door's paint is now chipping.

The door pitches open and a man in his 30s greets Anna with a smile. His business suit makes him stick out among the colorful crowd of costumes. Perhaps it *is* a costume. His tie is orange with bats scattered on it, blurring any assertion even more.

"Nice costume." His voice is soft beneath the bar's commotion.

"Thanks." Anna passes him, making sure that her shoulder comes in full contact with his, making damn sure he follows.

His fingers loosely slide around her wrist.

She stops. He is a little too sure of himself—too ballsy. She doesn't know if she likes that or not.

"Let me buy you a drink." His words carry a tone of apology over aggressiveness.

She looks at the bartender, Joe. If he is in a 'mood' tonight, she won't get served. She gently pulls away. "Sure."

They squeeze in at the bar. A clown sitting at the barstool beside him gets up. Mr. Businessman offers the seat and Anna takes it.

He leans over, whispering in her ear, "It isn't a costume, is it?"

"Nope." She looks him over and tugs on his tie. "Yours?"

He shakes his head, nope.

Bartender Joe places a mucho margarita in front of Anna. The dyed-orange liquid swirls in the glass and a plastic bat clinks against its sides. Joe starts to lean across the counter, getting ready to tell Anna all about how this guy is way too old for her, that she should be home, some crap like that.

She shakes her head at him. *Not now.* She turns her attention to the guy beside her and sips the margarita.

"Dos Equis," Mr. Businessman calls out to Joe, before redirecting his attention to Anna. "What's your name? I'm Parker."

He's actually asking for a name? She gives it. "Anna."

"Nice tattoo." His fingers brush the swollen skin surrounding the dragonfly, smearing the post-tattoo ointment. "My coworker has a dragonfly hanging in her office."

Anna downs half the margarita and checks her phone for the time.

"Am I that boring?" he says.

She looks up at him and smiles. "No, I have to be home soon."

"You don't look like a girl with a curfew."

She pauses, searching his eyes for a hint of insult. But he stays perfectly still, smiling. *God, he's got a great smile.*

"Did you drive here?" she asks.

"Yeah, my car is parked out back."

She grabs his hand, and he easily follows her out the back door. It slams shut behind them and the music dulls in the confinement of the walls.

He pulls out a set of keys and walks toward a blue BMW.

Anna hesitates. He makes it to the driver's side door. This could be the one—the ticket—into a better life. He turns his back to the Beamer's driver's side door, to the yellow, rusted passenger door of a Volkswagen Beetle. He opens it and rounds the back for its driver's seat.

Anna gets closer. The interior leather seats are in perfect condition. Parker climbs behind the wheel and she slides in beside him.

He leans the seat back a foot. "So—"

She presses her lips against his and climbs onto his lap. The weight of her lips pins his head to the headrest, keeping him from pulling away. His fingers slide into her hair and he pulls her harder against him. His lips pull away and move down her neck, toward the edge of the fresh tattoo. The fabric of his pants presses between her thighs. His fingers push up the edge of her skirt.

She grabs onto his hands. "Do you have a condom?"

He leans in and kisses her.

She absorbs that kiss as long as possible, pulls away, and gently slides back into the passenger seat.

The windows have fogged, softening the parking lot's glow.

She reaches for the door handle. There is no way she'll fuck him without protection. "It was nice to meet you, Parker."

"Wait...." He reaches for her shoulder. "Can we get a coffee sometime?"

Sixteenth Street—the café she works at—is only a few blocks away. But if he turns out to be that crazy-stalker type.... She can't afford having him show up at work. Anna forces the door open. It slams into the BMW, scraping the paint off its door. The wind nips at her skin. "How about you pick some up and we'll meet at the park?"

"Which park?" he asks.

"Chintimini Park. Nine o'clock tomorrow night."

"Do you want a lift somewhere?" he says.

The wind picks up, nudging her back into the Volkswagen. She wants nothing more than to climb in and drive off with the warm heater vent blowing through her fishnet stockings. She resists the urge, closes the door and walks away—down the alley that leads to the main street. The music, laughter, and roar of conversation fades as she heads east. She can hear the hum of Parker's car idling at the cross street behind her.

He turns west, leaving her in the cold autumn night.

It is a two mile walk home, but at least it isn't raining.

Headlights

The dim, flashing light of the trailer park sign appears in the distance. Rain sprinkles down as Anna crosses over the bridge, passes the bus stop, and turns onto the cul-de-sac.

Mrs. Quinn is throwing her husband's shit all over the yard again. If Anna keeps her eyes to the asphalt, she might be able to slip by unnoticed.

"You see this?" Mrs. Quinn shouts.

Crap. Anna never had a chance.

"This is what a piece of shit marriage looks like."

Anna picks up the pace.

"You fucking see this?" A beer bottle sways at Mrs. Quinn's side.

"Come 'n, babe." Mr. Quinn's words slur as his pathetic-ass scoops the clothes into a pile.

His wife pulls a hose from the side of their trailer, turns it on, and squirts him.

He screams.

Anna runs for home.

The lights are off. Mom and Jeremy must have gone to bed early. Mom called the café, making sure Anna had the day off tomorrow. It is Anna's last shot. The insurance won't cover any more doses of chemicals for a while. Anna reaches for her trailer key. *What's wrong with me?* The door is always unlocked. She stows the keys and turns the doorknob. Sure enough, the door opens.

Inside, a crappy late-night show spills subliminal messages across an empty living room. Anna takes off her sneakers and locks the door. A fresh pile of cupcakes sits in the middle of the counter. She passes them, heading for her bedroom. Inside, the streetlight shines through the pink dreamcatcher and rests on her bed.

It feels good to be home. She stands on tiptoe, peeking out the window at the Quinns'. They are still going at it. What chance did they have, anyway? Anna slides the dreamcatcher's feathers through her fingers until the frayed bottoms brush past. She can't help but think about all those kids her age whose parents buy them five-dollar lattes—they don't have bills to pay, to worry about. *They already have more of a chance than I will ever have.*

Anna flops down on the bed, staring at the ceiling, waiting for her life to change, for fate to grant her freedom from this shit hole.

In the distance, tires screech.

Lights zigzag across the ceiling.

Anna sits up.

The sound gets louder. The lights get brighter. She watches it dance across the ceiling, waiting for the approaching vehicle to crash through the wall and crush her. The wheels squeal and the bright lights cut across the ceiling, disappearing. An engine idles next door—at Brenda Martinez's place.

Her driveway is adjacent to Anna's side of the trailer. Every morning her car clunks into the driveway, waking Anna for work. She never comes home early. On holidays, she'll pull a double shift and stop by the café, always ordering a double espresso. On holidays, she tips big. Well, five bucks big, which is more than all the stingy high school kids leave.

Anna stands on her bed, staring out past the dreamcatcher's tattered feathers.

Brenda's 1990s Dodge Intrepid is in the driveway. The driver's door is open. The lights in her trailer flash on. She comes running out of the door with her arms full of clothes.

Socks and underwear fall like bread crumbs as she rounds the car, chucking them over the driver's seat to the back, then sprints back inside.

Headlights shot over the bridge in the distance. The vehicle skims the bus-stop and speeds toward the cul-de-sac.

Brenda's trailer lights go out.

The vehicle—a black Hummer—skids to a stop, blocking Brenda's driveway. The word Meadowlark ornaments its side door. An orange biohazard symbol is centered behind it, perfectly inline with its O.

A man wearing a black military uniform gets out. An identical Meadowlark logo is embroidered on his right sleeve. His eyes shoot toward Anna's window.

She plops down on the mattress so hard and fast she bounces off, hitting the wall.

Two deep male voices shift outside.

Anna picks herself up, presses her back against the wall, and stands tiptoe, peeking through the window. Nothing but the Hummer's left headlight is visible. Anna will have to climb back onto the bed to be able to see anything.

Bangs and thuds come from Brenda's trailer.

Anna glances up at the streetlight-stained ceiling and down at the pile of dirty laundry in the corner. *Screw it*. She climbs back onto the bed. The mattress sinks beneath her feet and it takes a second to stabilize. *Where are they?*

The Hummer still blocks the Dodge parked in the driveway. Brenda's trailer door is wide open, but it is completely dark inside. One of the men exits, walking backward, carrying something—someone. His arms are cupped beneath Brenda's armpits. The second man carries her feet. Brenda's fingers brush the porch steps as the men carry her to the Hummer, and throw her into the back.

Fuck.

The second man runs back to the trailer, pulling the door closed. He heads for the Dodge. His eyes shift to Anna's window.

She falls backward, letting her body bounce against the mattress. This time she settles into it and her whole body stiffens. Her heart thumps within her chest. *Shit. Shit. Shit.* She waits for the men to storm her trailer, to knock down the door, and carry her away from everything she has ever known.

A vehicle door slams shut.

Then another.

The headlights fade from her ceiling.

Prince Charming

One night of the year people dress up like freaks, drink to black out the night, and fill their heads with horror movies. One night out of the year Anna fits in.

Sunlight ripples across the ceiling. Anna can smell Mom even before she rolls over.

Mom's hair is wrapped in pink curlers. Black eyeliner fills the bags beneath her eyes.

Anna kisses her forehead. "Love ya, Mom."

Her mother's body sinks deeper into the worn mattress as she exhales, "Love you, my only."

Anna rolls off the bed and throws on the only piece of clothing worth anything—a white leather trench coat.

The kitchen is tranquil. The cupcakes are still stacked beside the cardboard box they came in.

Anna turns on the coffee pot.

The floorboards creak behind her.

"Eh, kiddo," Jeremy says, leaning in the hallway's threshold. He is the perfect stepdad for a trailer park. His wife-beater tank top is grey instead of white, and his typical football-print boxers are replaced with jack-o'-lanterns. He grabs a cupcake, offering it out. "You want a ride?"

Anna shakes her head, declining the cupcake. She can't eat anything for hours. And she doesn't want to talk about the procedure anymore. The last thing she needs is the awkward silence that a car ride would bring. Afterward, her coworker, Kelley, is picking her during lunch break. Anna doesn't have to worry about her bringing up anything. No way will she talk about it.

"Oh, right." Jeremy goes to bite into the moist cake, but stops, placing it back with the others. "Well, call me if you need anything."

"Jesus, Jeremy," Anna says. "It's only a colonoscopy."

His face flushes and pity begins to steal his smile.

She starts to laugh and points at him. "Shit, you're going to be fifty next year."

His pity breaks and a smile forces itself across his lips. It is so fun to mess with him.

The coffee machine beeps.

He pours the black liquid into an owl mug. "Milk? Sugar?"

"I'm only allowed to have jet black coffee."

He turns gently, handing over the mug. Steam dances in the cool room. He looks out the window over the sink. "Looks like the perfect All Hallows' Eve."

Clouds sweep the sun away. A silver sky frames the bright red maple tree outside. A leaf wiggles at the end of its farthest branch. The wind gusts, ripping it off, dragging it into the neighbor's yard—Megan Garret's lot. Her trailer is a hideous brown with yellow trim. She sits outside smoking a cigarette, staring into the kitchen window. *What a slut.* Her mom's Mexican boyfriend, Bernard, is outside stringing the orange lights. He is so nice—too nice to be associated with those two bitches.

"You going to feel up to decorating"—Jeremy kicks a pile of boxes beside the hallway—"after your appointment?"

"No. Put Mom to work. She could use some natural sunlight." Anna kisses his cheek and heads for the door. "Thanks, Dad."

She walks out, pulling the door closed. Coffee spills over the top of the cup and soaks the cuff of her sleeve, penetrating the white leather trench coat. She peeks over at Megan's trailer. Bernard's box of lights lay alone on the ground, blinking. *Coast's clear, thank God.* Anna sprints for the bus stop. *I don't need her shit today.* As long as Anna is out of shouting range before Megan comes out of the trailer, everything will be okay. Anna comes up on the stop.

Ms. Murphy is sitting on the far side of the bench.

Anna begins to say hello, but it isn't actually her. Anna's heart races. Her stomach knots. The person sharpens into a man —Mr. Perfect-smile, Dominic, from the café. He is here, right fucking here in Anna's trailer park.

"Hey," he says, "you look familiar."

"Yeah, I bet I do," she says.

"What?" he says.

"Really?" She can't believe it. For months he had been flirting with her. "You never called."

Out of the corner of her eye, a woman rounds the bench and slides onto his lap. Her ratty ponytail is half purple. Only one skank in the trailer park has hair like that. Megan shoves her tongue down his throat and he takes it like a champ, grabbing her fat ass. Her spandex legs spread wider, pressing harder against his lap. She pulls her lips from his, slowly licking them as she looks at me. "So, I hear you're getting fucked in the ass today."

Dominic leans back from her, cringing with the words.

Bitch is so intent on igniting a reaction from me.

The bus pops up over the hill.

Anna leans forward enough to lock eyes with Dominic. "I'm relieved you never called."

His lower lip drops.

Anna stands up and moves away from them. A breeze hits her cheek, dragging out the seconds before she'll be on the city chariot, taking her away from there.

The bus stops, its doors open, and Anna jumps in.

"You little b—" Megan's voice fades.

Anna hurries toward the back of the bus, away from the nagging voice trying to follow her up the steps. Anna's stomach gurgles, and pressure builds in her intestines. She takes the closest seat. The medical center is clear across town.

Dominic boards behind her, taking the seat across the aisle. His porcelain-white grin is as fake as his personality.

Asshole.

"You look beautiful today," he says.

Anna slides over into the window seat, leaning her cheek against the glass. Autumn air kisses the windowpane.

"Where you headed?" He slides into the seat beside her.

Her stomach churns and silent gas squeezes out of her bowels.

"Oh my God, what is that smell?" he says.

The cold window burns beneath her blushed cheeks.

The cushion shifts behind her with his departure, and emptiness returns to her side. Hurtful words whisper under his breath.

There is nothing she can do. It has been a long night of drinking chemicals, and the incident at Brenda's next door, had kept her up half the night. She is completely drained. Her fingers shake as she wipes the tear connecting her to the windowpane.

The café blurs into view for a moment before fading.

The bus jerks to a stop.

Dominic hops out and heads for the BMW still in the bar's parking lot. He stops before opening the driver's side door, staring at the scrape and dent in it. It's large enough to be seen all the way from the curb. His hands fly out to the side as he throws a fit. "What the —"

The bus pulls away and Anna sinks back into the seat, smiling. The fact that it was his car she scratched last night, made the whole day worth it.

COLONOSCOPY

THE REST OF TOWN BLURS BY AS THE BUS HEADS FOR the medical center. In no time, Anna is naked, lying between privacy curtains in a long line of gurneys. The sterile air of the medical facility hits her neck and blows down the open back of her hospital gown. Non-skid socks wrap her feet and a net secures her hair to prevent contamination of the facility.

She leans back into the pillow. A 50-something male is wheeled by. A young male intern smiles at her as he walks in the opposite direction. Her cheeks blaze. This is the last place she wants to pick up a boyfriend.

A loud fart sounds out behind the right curtain.

"Here, try lying on your side," a woman's voice filters through the cotton wall. "Bring your knees in."

A second loud fart cuts through the still room.

Oh, God.

The hot intern returns. "How are you doing,"—he grabs the chart off the end of the bed—"Ms. Page?"

"Okay," barely makes it past the ball in her throat. *Hell, no! He can't be the one assisting my procedure.*

He steps closer, pulling the stethoscope from his neck. The scent of musty pine needles sweeps into Anna's next breath, as he presses the stethoscope to her chest. She can't swallow another breath. Her heart races. He listens, smiles, and jots down a few numbers, patting her leg before walking away.

Her fingers have twisted together and sweat has pooled in her palms. She untangles them, wiping the sweat onto the sheet.

"Are you ready?" Dr. Kirstin Mullin steps out from behind the curtain. She looks thinner in scrubs.

Anna isn't ready.

Dr. Mullin rounds the bed and pats Anna's hand. "We'll find out what's going on."

Another college guy rounds the curtain from the left.

Anna's heart jumps, sticking in her throat.

He is skinny and tall, in his early 20s. His posture reminds her of a jackrabbit standing up on its hind legs, trying to nibble on the leaves of a bush.

Adrenaline shots through Anna's veins and eases. She is uncomfortable with a guy being present for the procedure. *Why should I care if some dude sees my ass?* She forces a smile and he perks up. *Jesus.*

He unlocks the gurney and pushes it down the hallway, into a small room. "Roll onto your left side."

Anna does as instructed and the blanket slides off her bare ass.

Dr. Mullin pulls the sheet back up. "So, you're going to feel all warm and fuzzy, and then you'll fall asleep."

The assistant, Jackrabbit, slides a thick needle into the top of Anna's right hand.

"How you doing, Anna?" Dr. Mullin says. "Are you feeling sleepy yet?"

"It kind'a hurts," says Anna.

Dr. Mullin rushes around the bed and grabs Anna's hand. "Jack, you missed the vein."

Anna's heart pounds. *Great.*

Dr. Mullin pulls the needle out and repositions it.

Warmth floods Anna. *Jack—ha—that's funny.* The room goes fuzzy and she falls down the rabbit hole.

Faint Lines

A PEACH CIRCLE FILLS THE TELEVISION SCREEN. ANNA'S eyelids blink, slowly. The cream color tunnels into a defined image of her colon. *What the—?* Something is still in her butt. She moves and the object sways, tightening her gluts. *What the hell?*

A faint "shush" comes from the floor behind her.

What the...?

"Don't move," says Jackrabbit.

Anna freezes. Her heart pounds into a race.

Something whacks against the door's glass window.

JULIE EMBERS

Anna's heart jumps. Or at least she thinks she jumps. *Shit.* The sedative hangs heavy in her veins and dulls her consciousness.

Silence takes hold of the minutes.

Cold fingers wrap around her hip, tightly grip her, and hold firm. The object dislodges, and the television screen goes black.

Anna starts to cover her mouth, but stops halfway. The needle in her hand wiggles, digging into the walls of her vein.

Jackrabbit slowly stands up beside her, pulls the IV out, and scoops her off the gurney, sliding her down into his arms, onto the floor.

A scream rips through the hallway's air.

He cups her mouth and pins his arms around her.

The scream repeats, digging deeper into Anna's heart.

What the fuck was that? What's happening?

He whispers into her ear, "There's someone out there"—a third scream pierces the door—"killing people."

Silence takes over.

He removes his hand from her mouth. "You're going to be out of it for a while. I'll get you out of here."

Anna takes one look at him and presses her lips together to restrain the laughter.

Something slams into the door again.

Anna presses her back against Jack's chest. Things aren't funny anymore.

His arms tighten around her.

A bloody handprint streaks down the window to the hallway.

The Last Day

JACK NUDGES ANNA TO MOVE—TO STAND UP—BUT SHE can't. Her knees won't budge. He slides out from behind her. The string in the back of her hospital gown loosens, falling open.

Blush burns into her cheeks.

His fingers brush her back to tie a bow. He crouches beside the door, resting his hand on its knob. With each inhale, his shoulder blades expand. He glances back. "You ready?"

Hell no. She is not ready for any of this shit. She pushes herself to stand.

He offers a hand and she takes it. He turns the doorknob. Her heart swells. The door cracks an inch. Something slams into it from the other side and Anna falls. Jackrabbit clenches the doorknob, saving him from landing on top of her .

A face appears on the other side of the door's window. The hot intern from earlier presses the side of his face against the glass, trying to see the floor.

Jack sinks to the side, hiding from view, leaning back against the door. It falls open, knocking the intern to the floor. The door ricochets off the hallway wall as the hot intern rocks like a turtle, trying to get up. Jack freezes. Anna pushes off the floor, grabs Jack's shirt, and yanks him with her as she sprints for the hallway. *I'm not going to die today.*

The intern makes it onto his side. Drool, pink with blood, drips off his lips. His left front tooth is broken in half. Red, swollen veins encase the yellow balls in his eye sockets. His fingers dig into the tile—sliding through the drool—pushing to get up. Fluorescent-green snot leaks from his nose, pooling onto his upper lip.

Anna digs the rubber of her socks into the floor, running for the recovery room, rounding the corner.

A man is in the way of the exit. A hospital gown hangs off his dislocated shoulder. He steps forward. Blood drips onto the floor behind him. Whatever is wrong with the intern has spread to the patient.

Jack's fingernails dig into Anna's skin as he screams behind her.

She jerks her hand away from his, looking back at him.

The intern's bloody fingers slide down Jack's hair, forming a fist. His cracked tooth chomps down into the flesh of Jack's neck.

Anna runs. She runs at the guy guarding the door.

He grunts, lurching faster. She zigzags like a kid playing tag. He reaches out, grabbing the shoulder of her hospital gown. The loose strings unravel. It falls to the floor. *Screw it*. She is naked and it doesn't matter. She shoves the door open and spills out into the lobby.

A woman with two children sits at the far end of the room, tapping her knee. A businessman sits beside the entrance, laughing at the cellphone in his hand. Opposite him, is a security guard and a secretary blabbing appointment times on the phone.

The door bangs against the wall.

The mother looks up and her mouth falls open. Anna can feel her eyes shoot from the fresh tattoo on her breast to the Brazilian cut between her thighs. The mother gasps, covering the children's eyes. The businessman glances away from his phone to the mother. The phone slides out of his hand, bounces off his lap, and thumps to the floor.

The secretary stops mid-mumble. The phone drifts away from her ear. Standing, she says, "Ma'am—

The security guard pops off his seat and heads for Anna with his hands out like she is going to hurt somebody. "Ma'am, stay right there."

Anna can hear the tearing of flesh behind her. Jack's screams reach into the lobby. The security guard freezes for a moment. Anna runs at him—for the only way out. His eyes shoot past her to the recovery room beyond and his body shifts past her. A gust of air, trailing him, brushes her skin. The secretary yells as Anna rams the door open and crosses the barrier into the outside world.

The guard's screams escape the medical center just before the door swings shut behind Anna.

A yellow leaf grazes her shoulder as it gusts by.

She runs—gets the hell out of there. Gooseflesh ripples across her skin. She heaves all the air from her lungs. An older woman, walking into the adjoining building, stops and stares at her. A security cruiser comes speeding around the parking lot, heading toward Anna. *Crap.* She is naked and fleeing the scene of a crime. She can flag them down or run.

The cruiser skids to a stop, walling off the path in front of her. A chubby man with wide eyes is stuffed behind it's steering wheel. He throws open his door and plants a foot.

Anna runs. Nothing good comes from talking to the cops.

He yells, "Stop!"

He could have a gun, pulling it out of his holster and pointing it at her. She cuts down a sidewalk and heads for a side street. She isn't going down for some fucked-up shit.

He yells louder, "Stop!"

A white Volkswagen van stops at the curb in front of her.

She jumps in.

The security guard rams into the side door, pounding against the window.

The van takes off.

Anna stares at the glove box, attempting to gasp a full breath of air. She turns to look at the driver and whacks her face against a surfboard. "Ouch."

"Oh, man," a guy says. "Are you okay?"

Anna's heartbeat spikes. *Crap.* Only a pervert would pick up a naked chick running from the cops. *What does he look like?* Looks say everything about how creepy a guy is. She tries to look over the board, but can't see anything but flyaway hair, maybe blonde. *Damnit.* She grabs the door handle, holding it tight, moving her knees closer to the door incase of a needed escape. Her socks stick to the floor. Empty protein-bar wrappers crinkle at the movement.

"Hold on," he says.

The van slams to a stop. Anna's butt slides off the seat and her elbow hits the glove box.

An old lady pushes a walker over the white lines of a crosswalk in front of them.

"There's a poncho on the floor back there," he says, "if you can reach it."

Anna looks back beneath the surfboard. A piece of fabric that looks more like a Mexican rug than clothes lays on an orange shag carpet. She leans under the board, reaching for it.

"Damn, girl," he says.

Shit. Her whole body tightens and she bangs her head on the board. "Ouch." She grabs the poncho and slides back into the passenger seat, sinking a little deeper. "Who the hell do you think you are?"

The old lady waves from the curb.

"Chill," he says, waving back as the van jerks forward. "I'm just saying, you look good. That's all. So, where you headed?"

She slides the poncho on, leans back, crosses her arms, and watches the world creep past the window. She wants to go home, but doesn't want him to know where she lives. *He could be some sick pervert. Some deadbeat hippie who—*

He pulls over to the side of the road. "I don't mind dropping you somewhere, but driving without purpose is only burning gas."

A crescendo of sirens comes from the wrong direction.

"The café on Sixteenth," blurts from her lips. She needs somewhere close—safe. A location he could give when the cops strangle it out of him.

The van pulls back into traffic and the driver stays silent the rest of the way there. The blurred lines of the curb drift into replaying thoughts of Brenda's limp fingers brushing the steps of her trailer last night—the two men in black lugging her to their Hummer. *Something's not right.*

The van stops out front of the café. The guy hops out and rounds the back of the van.

Anna leans to catch his reflection in the side view, but he already has the door handle, pulling it open. He isn't much older than her. His hair is twisted into thick, ratty dreadlocks. They are a sandy blonde, but the roots are darker. Otherwise, he looks pretty normal. He offers a hand and steps back, giving her room to move around him. "I'm James."

She stares down at his hand. A gust of air pushes through the threads of the poncho. *What am I doing?* She looks down at the hospital socks, soaking against the sidewalk.

"You gotta get out of here." The words spill out of her mouth before she can evaluate them. *Yes. I've got to get out of here. At least for a little while.* "Head for the coast—something. There … there was an attack at the hospital."

He steps closer. "Are you going to be okay?"

What? She looks at him. A tear drips down her cheek. *I'm not crazy.* She wipes it off as if it were a hornet. *There had been an attack. Hadn't there?* She searches his eyes for something— something to verify that this is real, not a fucking sedated dream —something to prove she is awake.

His eyes search hers for any evidence of fucking sanity.

Anna gives a faint "thanks" and makes for the café door, tugging the edge of the poncho down over her butt.

The bell jingles. The wind hits it again, begging for another ring.

She looks at the farthest booth first. There is no old man sitting beneath the mosaic dragonfly. The pieces of mirror sparkle as she walks through the mid-day rush.

Kelley is taking orders at the counter. She catches sight of Anna and her eyes grow wide. Anna's colonoscopy wasn't supposed to be finished for another hour. She glances back over her shoulder to the prep area. Ms. Tumult must be in.

The café ignites with whispers as Anna descends deeper, passing the counter into sanctuary.

Ms. Tumult is in the back, lugging a bag of coffee beans from the walk-in freezer. Cold air spills across the floor and disappears. She grunts and groans over its weight. Her stance is distorted and groans too deep.

No. She can't be .... Maybe it is an infection, some type of virus. Anna steps back. *No. Not her, not here.*

Ms. Tumult turns her head, looking straight at Anna. "What are you doing here?"

Anna's heart swells in relief.

Her teeth aren't stained with blood. Her eyes aren't swollen and yellow. They shine and light up with surprise at the sight of Anna. "Why haven't you called me back? I tried your mom five times to see how things were going."

Ms. Tumult refuses to call Mom by her name. Anna doesn't know if it is because of something back when they were in high school together, or if its just because she can't remember Mom's name.

"I ran out of minutes," says Anna. *That should smooth it over.*

Ms. Tumult's eyes narrow, giving away the fact that Kelley spilled the beans about picking Anna up from the medical center. Her crinkled lips press together as she tries to restrain the urge to drill Anna about Mom not going.

"I'm gonna use the bathroom," says Anna.

Ms. Tumult looks her over and Anna can see it sink in: what Anna's wearing, the fact that her naked butt is almost hanging out the bottom of a stranger's poncho. She says, "What happened?"

Anna tugs the edge of the poncho down, trying to force another inch out of the fabric, shaking her head and lifting her shoulders. "I don't know."

She runs over, hugging Anna.

Anna starts to freakin' cry like a weak, pathetic girl.

Ms. Tumult's fingers slide through Anna's hair, pulling off the medical hairnet. Each inhale tastes like baby powder. She shushes Anna, pushing her away—holding Anna out from her. "Go get cleaned up."

Anna sucks back her tears and makes for the bathroom. Inside, the large mirror hanging over the sink captures a girl who should be walking through high school corridors, laughing and hanging out with other girls her age. She sits down on the toilet. Most girls her age don't have to help pay the bills. They spend all their time on cell phones and aren't bleeding out their asses. She leans against the wall and stares at the mirror, avoiding her reflection, focusing on a crack in the tile mortar.

She doesn't know how much time passes, but Ms. Tumult is tapping on the door. Anna isn't even sure how long she has been there.

"Hey, I'm leaving some clothes out here for you." Ms. Tumult's voice fades, followed by footsteps.

Anna cracks the door and peeks out. A pile of clothes lays outside on the floor. She grabs them and shuts the door. They are top-of-the-line, something the popular kids wear to fit in. The shirt is white, thin. She slides out of the poncho and into the blouse. The rayon fabric rubs against her tender chest. She pulls on a pair of tight black pants, not bothering to look in the mirror —give it a reason to judge her, scream 'poser.'

She opens the door and glances back at the mirror. *Poser.* She grabs the poncho off the floor and pulls it on, entering the back prep area.

The freezer door flies open. Ms. Tumult backs out of the walk-in as she drags another bag of beans out.

Kelley's voice drifts around the espresso machine from the front register, taking an order.

Anna should tell her—them—what happened. *What if I am crazy?* Ms. Tumult went out on a limb hiring her. Anna is supposed to be in high school for Christ's sake, not working to pay the bills.

The café phone rings.

Anna's heart jumps.

Ms. Tumult's cell phone *beeps* from her purse nearby on the prep counter. Anna should have told her. Now she'll hear it from someone else. Ms. Tumult drops the bag and goes for the phone, stopping to nudge the freezer door shut. A "hello" passes her lips and her eyes shoot toward Anna, who dips into the storefront out of earshot.

Anna doesn't want to face Ms. Tumult, be interrogated, and spend the day detained by police.

Kelley races around like a hamster without a wheel: taking orders, steaming espressos, shuffling money into the register.

The café phone stops ringing.

Everything about the packed café would suggest that all is right with the world. But it isn't. The café has never been this busy. There are so many people. Some stand in the aisles around tables, others lean against the wall beside the booths.

Kelley stops in front of Anna, turning her back to the mob of people. "Hey, I thought you said eleven o'clock?"

Everyone's chatter, laugher, idle conversations continue on like nothing has happened—like a man didn't just try to kill her … kill someone. He killed people.

Kelley's face changes, her shoulders drop. "Shit. Anna, I'm sorry. How'd—"

Anna draws her eyes away from Kelley's. It isn't fair. Kelley has her own flat by campus, all four years of college paid for her, and she isn't dying. It isn't her fault. Anna can't hold it against her. Kelley has always tried to be nice: commenting on Anna's outfits, but never the worn texture or the faded fabric and torn strings. Anna grabs the next order up, clears her throat, and draws the tears back in. "Yeah."

Kelley stays with her back to the crowd, letting it fade into another world. "Anna…."

"I'm fine. We can talk about it later." What would it change, anyway? Any second, news about the incident at the hospital will spread over social media like wildfire. Avoiding it now will spare Anna more time. If it is even real. It is only a matter of time before the cops find her.

An hour later, the last order hits the counter. Anna collapses against the espresso machine, leaning on the register, thankful not to be moving.

"I see the clothes fit," Kelley says, grabbing a 20-ounce macchiato. "But why are you wearing that hideous rug over it?"

"I don't have a bra."

"Girl, that's the whole point. Trust me. You'll get way more tips without one." She turns away from the customers and rubs one breast. "If there's a really hot guy," she moves her hand and the nipple shoots out like an eraser, "you might get more than a tip."

Society repressed female urges for so long. Anna feels the smoldering ashes awaken, but she isn't ready to sell her body to quench it. She feels the need as much as Kelley does. She just isn't a slut about it. Well ...

"So, do you have any plans for tonight?" Kelley says, sipping the macchiato.

Anna imagines the whole police force standing on the porch of her trailer, banging on the door, forcing themselves into her home, waiting in the kitchen for her as they devour the pile of cupcakes. Jeremy would be stringing lights in his boxers. Megan's slutty ass would try to find some reason to breach the property line for intel.

The café bell jingles and cold air sweeps in, tearing the image from Anna's grasp.

Kelley takes another sip of coffee. "I'm"—loud footsteps approach the counter from behind her—"having a party."

Two men in black uniforms—Meadowlark Agents— approach the counter.

Shit. Anna looses her balance and leans against the espresso machine, catching the counter's edge.

Kelley glances back at Anna and pinches both nipples, ready to work her magic. Her voice raises to an excited pitch, "May I help you?"

The shorter of the two men leans against the counter, staring at the two points of her blouse.

The second agent slides a photograph across the counter. His icy-blue eyes meet Anna's, shooting icicles through her veins. "Have you seen this girl?"

The photograph captures a girl about Anna's age with blue eyes and long blonde curls, sitting at a booth in a café. A piece of the mosaic dragonfly's tail hangs over her shoulder in the background. *It's this café.*

Anna glances over the man's shoulder, at the dragonfly booth, and follows the photographer's angle —to the front window. *There's no way to capture that same angle, unless ....* *It's a surveillance photograph.*

He follows her eyes. "Well...?"

Anna recognizes the girl in the photo. How could she not? The girl always meets that guy, Dominic, on Thursdays.

"Asshole," says Anna.

"What?" says the man, raising his voice.

Crap. I said that out loud.

His partner straightens up, staring at Anna too. His hand moves to his belt—to the hilt of a samurai sword.

A freakin' samurai sword? "Oh, sorry. Not you ... I was...." Anna shoves a piece of hair behind her ear and scrapes the photograph from the counter. "Nope. Never seen her."

Kelley leans over in a way that presses her breasts together, while looking at the picture. "Isn't she one of the regulars?"

His blue eyes narrow.

Crap. Anna pretends to look at the photograph again. "Maybe you're right."

"Have you seen her today?" he says, keeping his stare.

"Hey, Anna—" Ms. Tumult steps out from the back. "What's going on here?" She approaches the group, taking the photograph out of Anna's hand. "What's this?"

"Ma'am," Mr. Blue Eyes says, "have you seen this woman before?"

Ms. Tumult smiles and looks up at him. "Are you gentlemen buying anything?"

Blue Eyes gives his partner a nod.

Anna's heart sinks. They aren't going away anytime soon. She has to get out of here. If she runs, they'll hunt her. She can feel it: their desire to force answers out of her—drag her off like they did with Brenda.

His partner starts rattling off a long list of items.

Ms. Tumult sets the photograph on the counter. "She comes in every Thursday with that boyfriend of hers—"

So he is her boyfriend. Why was he at Megan's? What a piece of shit.

"Any other days?" the agent asks.

Ms. Tumult looks at Anna.

Anna's palms sweat. Her hands shake. The walls of her stomach quiver.

His partner pauses from the order he is placing. He looks at Ms. Tumult. "And the five-layer cocoa bean cake."

Ms. Tumult's eyes light up. She paid $100 for it next door. That alone was a $400 profit. "Tell you what," she says, sliding the photograph back across the counter. "Next time she's in, I'll have one of the girls ring ya."

Blue Eyes stares at Anna, pocketing the picture. "Deal. But if I don't get the call"—his fingers slide to the holster—"I won't be buying shit next time I come in here."

Anna falls off balance, leaning against Ms. Tumult.

Ms. Tumult wipes a lock of hair from Anna's face and puts an arm around her. "Now if you'll excuse me."

Kelley continues jotting down the list of items as Ms. Tumult guides Anna to the backroom.

Her phone rings.

She ignores it, sitting down across from Anna. "What was that about?"

"What?" Anna says.

"Why did you lie to those—those men?" Ms. Tumult asks.

Something isn't right: the men at Brenda's, the clinic, and now this. If Anna tells her, she'll think she's crazy. Maybe she is. Maybe she's still at the doctor's, knocked out, dreaming a nightmare—a life she can't get away from. Anna shrugs. Maybe she'll wake up soon.

Ms. Tumult's phone stops ringing then starts again.

"You might want to get that," Anna says. Right about now the news will be blowing up with reports of the clinic's attack. It won't be long before the real cops come to question her. They'll try home first, then here.

Ms. Tumult answers her phone, spins, and stares at Anna. "Yes. She's right here."

A Ride Home

Mom actually tracked Anna down, wondering why the hell she wasn't home, resting. Ms. Tumult calmed her down and offered to give Anna a ride home—more like insisted.

Anna keeps her head pressed up against the window the entire way. Ms. Tumult flips through radio stations, stopping on some Michael Bolton crap. Anna really isn't in the mood for all this bullshit about unrequited love.

An overcast sky blocks out the noon sun.

Ms. Tumult pulls into the trailer park, inching her shoulders up to her ears, trying to shield herself from the low-lifes.

Brenda's Dodge is still in her driveway. The Quinns' trailer is quiet. Ms. Murphy is in her yard, picking at the garden boxes.

Ms. Tumult shifts in her seat. Anytime she visits, it is an in-and-out job. She stops at the edge of Anna's driveway.

Jeremy's Camaro is gone. Just like Mom, to call in a panic and disappear to score something.

Anna opens the passenger door, swings out her legs, and stares at the soggy hospital socks.

"You..." Ms. Tumult shifts into park, "you..."

"It's cool. I'll be okay. See you tomorrow." Anna hops out and shuts the door. Ms. Tumult hadn't anticipated no one being home, but Anna had. It isn't a big deal, not usually. Anna looks at the trailer door. There is something wrong with the world. She can feel it, like a wave rippling beneath the water, approaching the coastline, coming quicker.

Ms. Tumult lowers the car window.

Anna leans in. "Thanks."

She stuffs her concern behind a smile.

Anna taps on the roof and steps back.

Ms. Tumult drives away and Anna ascends the steps, pulling out her keys. Her hands shake. She wishes they'd stop doing that. She goes to stick the key into the door, but it is cracked open. Her heart jerks. *Crap.* She looks down the road.

Ms. Tumult's Mercedes is long gone. The cul-de-sac is quiet. Ms. Murphy hums softly, picking at the garden bed. Anna wants to go say hi, ask her to come in with her, hold her fucking hand like a baby. *Screw it.* She throws open the door. "Mom? Jeremy?"

The image of the hospital—the unquenchable hunger in the hot intern's eyes as he tore into Jackrabbit's neck—shoots through her thoughts. She scans the living room and kitchen. Jeremy's cupcake from earlier had offset the pile, smearing it's icing into the one beside it. The box of Halloween lights has moved from the hallway entrance to the front door. Anna takes a step inside. *Mom...?* She takes another step and looks for something—something she can defend herself with if needed. The umbrella. It's behind her, in a large bowl opposite the Halloween lights. She grabs it. Its tip is a long point—something to stab into an intruder's eye socket.

The hallway is dark. All she wants is to lay down in her bed. She can sprint straight for it, dodging anything coming from Mom's room down the hallway.

All these thoughts are making things worse. There isn't anything to be scared of. It was just one attack, one isolated incident. But the front door had been open.

She sprints through the kitchen. *Halfway there.* Her heart is about to burst. She heaves all the air from her lungs and keeps going, through the darkness, until she makes it into her room. She slams the door shut and throws its lock. She can't stop whatever is coming, but she can lock herself in her room and forget about the world for a while—or at least until it comes knocking.

And it will come knocking.

MOMENTS

MOM PLEADS FROM THE OTHER SIDE OF ANNA'S bedroom door, "Anna? *Only?* Baby, please let me in."

Is she crying? Anna jumps out of bed. The room spins. *Fuck.* She is lightheaded. She weaves in the dark, feeling for the doorknob, gets it, and pulls it open.

Mom falls into her. She reeks of beer and her words are slurred, "Why you lock your door? Sorry, I..." She throws her arms around Anna. "I fucked up. I'm such a horrible mom."

Anna runs her fingers through her mother's hair and kisses her forehead. "Stop being dramatic."

"Why do you hate me?" says Mom.

"I don't hate you—"

"Why'd you lock your door?" She stumbles out of Anna's arms and flops onto the bed.

"The front door was..." Anna glances toward the kitchen, "unlocked. I thought..." She glances back at her mom.

She has passed out.

Anna picks a thin comforter off the floor. It is comprised of various square patterns. When Anna was little, she liked to pretend her mother had cut each one out for her and they'd spent hours laughing and telling stories while piecing it together. Anna pulls it over her mother, tucking those imaginary moments away. The cotton between the sheets of fabric had withered away when Anna was young, but it is still her favorite.

She grabs a hoodie off the floor and pulls it on as she heads for the front door. The clock above the kitchen window has been stuck at two o'clock for as long she can remember. The microwave digits glow 9:30. *Great.* Kelley's party started over a half hour ago. Anna just needed a drink, to blur the day's events and rid the fear from her thoughts, or at least drown them out for a while. *How the hell am I going to get there at this time of night?* She hurries out the front door.

"Hey, where are you going?" Jeremy says, popping his head out over the roof. He is standing at the top of a ladder, hanging Halloween lights. "Why was your door locked?"

Anna halts and plops down on the steps.

He drops the lights and climbs down.

She can't tell him about what happened at the clinic. If it had happened, it would have been on the news, he would have said something. Maybe she had imagined it all. She glances over her shoulder at Brenda's. Her car still sits in the driveway. "You know you've always been..." *Am I really having this conversation? Fine.* "You've always been cool, ya know?"

He comes over, resting a hand on her shoulder. "Did you get the results?"

She doesn't want to talk about her fucking bloody ass. *Something is wrong. Something's seriously wrong with the world. I can feel it.* She shakes her head, stands up, and hugs him—hugs him like it is the last time she will ever see him.

He pats her back and pulls away. Too much affection makes him uncomfortable.

She stands up and heads for the bus stop.

"You want a ride?" he asks.

She turns around. "Dad?"

"Yeah?"

"Take care of Mom."

"Anna?"

Yeah? A breeze blows, pulling at her hair.

"Peace, love, and happiness." He makes a peace sign, kisses it, and blows it at her.

That always makes her smile. It is the only way he can say the world "love" to her. Since she was little, he wiped her boogies, made her breakfast, and bought her first horror book. He never told her he loved her, and she never needed his confirmation. She makes a peace sign back and blows a kiss, then turns and walks down the street in the dark—where the lamplight doesn't reach.

Bad Decisions

Fog settles in while Anna sits at the bus stop. Headlights shoot over the bridge in the distance and cut through the settled clouds. Night air carries the chill of winter's approach. The bus's brakes screech before her. An owl hoots in a nearby tree. Anna shudders and shakes the chill from her spine, hopping onto the bus.

A couple is making out in the back, and an old man sits three rows behind the driver on the left. Anna pulls the hood of her sweatshirt up and takes the opposite side, halfway back.

The bus kicks into drive and takes off toward town. Butterflies swarm Anna's stomach at the thought of Parker—the business guy she is supposed to be going to meet. She should have worn lace panties. It doesn't matter. The park will be dark, and they won't be on long enough for him to care. The reflection of a girl who knows better, who has self-respect, looks back at her. What does she know about love? Anna doesn't plan on being a soft pillow for some guy to lay down his head.

The dude sucking face in the back starts coughing.

Guess they're not sucking face now.

The bus jerks to the next stop.

The guy coughs again. His girlfriend mumbles, concerned. He shushes her between coughs that get louder as he stands. Anna glances back. He is two steps back from her, hunched over. A chill pulses through her spine as he passes. His girlfriend hikes down a slutty maid costume as they pass. He makes it to the old man, leans on his seat hunched over, and hacks into his hand. The slutty maid rubs his back. He nudges her away and grabs onto the seat across from the old man, pushing himself forward. They disappear down the steps.

Anna presses her cheek to the cold windowpane. Outside, the guy is still hacking, leaning against the bus stop sign. The bus pulls away, shifting the lamplight. Anna's reflection washes away the couple. Anna knows she is as much of a slut as the girlfriend, but she doesn't care. The bus glides down the same monotonous route. Another chill shoots up Anna's spine. She whips around, making sure no one else is sitting in the back, hiding. *All I want to do is forget the day.* The seats are empty. *Just have a drink and find a good time, disappear from this world for a few hours.* She faces forward.

The old man's whole body is twisted, eyes wide at the seat across from him. No one is there.

What if whatever happened at the colonoscopy is real? What if the old fucker sprints back here and tears my fucking throat out?

His chest rises, long and slow.

Quit it. She's freaking herself out. It was just the drugs they gave her. The cops never showed up. Who the hell knows if it was real. She looks down at the designer pants—Kelley's pants. She ran naked from the cops, but the memory is a blur. *If it is cancer, can it do that? Mess up my brain?*

The bus stops.

She needs something to shift her thoughts.

"Hey, Pops!" the driver says, peering in the rearview mirror.

The old man keeps his eyes on the seat.

The driver bites his lip, creating a loud whistle.

The old man stands, staring at the seat. He stops at the stairs and looks back at the seats. His eyes shift to Anna. Then he is gone, down the same steps as all the others.

The bus takes off and the driver looks back at her. "What stop, love?"

"Chintimini Park."

The bus blows past the next few stops. The driver slows at each one, making sure no one is running from the bustling bars, and keeps on going. The next one is it. He doesn't care when Anna stands, taking to the aisle , making her descent while the bus is still moving. The tires skid to a stop. Momentum jerks her forward, then back. *What the hell was the old man looking at?* She approaches the seat he had been sitting in.

A bloody handprint drips down the canvas, dragging the fingerprints toward the floor.

Oh, my God. Anna stumbles faster down the aisle, covering her mouth, restraining a scream. She bumps into the driver.

He says something—maybe apologizing for his shitty stopping.

Anna stumbles down the steps and jumps out.

He mumbles something else and pulls the doors closed, taking off, leaving her in the fog.

Her heart races. *The bus.* She glances back. The brake lights smolder into the layer of cloud. *Shit.* She crumples the cuff of her sleeve and tucks her hands in her armpits. *This was a stupid idea.*

She glances back down the road, waiting for the slutty-maid's boyfriend to come stumbling down the street, ready to rip her head off. *Too many goddamn zombie movies.* She pulls the hoodie tighter and walks down the sidewalk. Streetlights cut through the fog enough for her to see the park sign and a row of benches, but the play structure is hidden in the blanket of clouds. She'll give Parker 20 minutes.

The air is colder than anticipated. Drops of dew have gathered on the bench. If she sits, her pants will get soaked. The wind seeps through the threads of her hoodie.

Headlights pierce the fog and turn into the parking lot.

Her heart races. Parker is more than a decade older than her. *What am I doing?*

The headlights go out.

What am I doing?

The silhouette of the vehicle isn't a Volkswagen Beetle. It is a sedan. A guy gets out and walks toward her.

Crap. She shoves her hands in the hoodie pocket, attempting to look more badass than stranded.

The guy looks about 23, maybe older. His cheeks are sunken in. A faded flannel shirt hangs over his boney shoulders. His jeans have holes in them. Of course that doesn't mean anything. Kelley paid top dollar for a pair of jeans with holes and tears in them. Apparently it is 'in' fashion, but something tells her this guy doesn't know that.

"Hey, doll-face," he says, stopping three feet away.

If she runs or shows any fear, he will be able to tell. Animals can sense it. And by the looks of it, this guy has been living solely on animal instinct his whole life. Anna stands up straighter. "What's up?"

A grin pulls at the edges of his lips. "Whatcha doing all alone out here in the dark? Shouldn't you be at home playing with Barbies?"

Shit. She knows where this is going. Most of the

underground guys are decent, but a handful never escaped the beatings of childhood and the rape from their uncles. Anna's fists clench. She wore her Doc Martin boots, but couldn't afford the ones with steel toes. *Shit.* Even if she kicks him in the nuts, he might not go down. *Something … I need something to make him know … I need more time, something until Parker shows up and fixes all this.*

"You want a suck or handjob?" she asks.

The corners of his lips draw up into a smile. "I got some cocaine back at the car."

Anna never touches the hard stuff. Too many people on her block had come and gone from the hard shit. It really fucked them up and destroyed their families—destroyed everything they ever were or would be.

"How about a line for a hand job?" She presses her tongue against the inside of her cheek. "I've got these sores…"

He pulls his head back in disgust, yet nods toward the car, leading her toward it.

Fuck, that didn't work. Her heart pounds so fiercely that each breath is cut short. *I should run, but it has to be the right time.* She had played tag enough as a kid to know she isn't the fastest runner.

He opens the passenger door like a gentleman and she has to hold back a laugh. Maybe in another life he would have been a real sweet guy. Poverty is like a drug addiction. You're never really free from it.

If she can get him to the other side of the car, create a barrier between them, she could get a head start. She slides into the seat, leaving the door open as he rounds the back and climbs into the driver's side—belt buckle and zipper already undone. He takes out a vial from his pocket, dumps a small pile of white powder on the dashboard, pulls a razor-blade from the center console, and hands Anna a rolled dollar bill as he cuts the pile into lines.

"Do you like it fast or slow?" Anna asks, glancing back at the park bench. She could round the benches and make off into the fog. *Should I hide in the playground or keep going ... sprint to fucking town?*

"You gonna shut the damn door?" he asks.

Anna smiles. He has no idea what is coming. She leans closer to the dash, takes a deep breath and blows the line of coke into dust.

He starts yelling, "What the fuck? You stupid—"

Anna turns, jumps out of the car, and runs as fast and as hard as she can.

"Fucking bitch," he yells. He follows in hot pursuit, gaining on her.

She sprints for the bench. There is no time to go around. If she doesn't hop over it, he will cut her off. Anna goes for it, jumps on the bench and flings a leg over it. Her other foot slips. She crashes over the bench, falling on the cement behind it. Her left cheek slams first, scraping against the concrete.

He grabs the back of her head and yanks her off the ground, pushing her stomach up against the back of the bench. "You stupid cunt."

Headlights pierce the parking lot. A yellow Volkswagen Beetle parks beside the sedan. It is Parker.

Thank God.

The piece-of-shit behind Anna tightens his grip in her hair, bending her over the bench. She tries to lift her eyes to the parking lot, but he slams her face down into the metal bench.

"Hey!" says Parker. It sounds like he is running toward them. "What the fuck do you think you're doing?"

The piece-of-shit pushes harder against Anna's head.

She can see through the metal of the bench.

The asshole slides his free hand behind him and pulls out a knife.

Fuck.

He holds it out in front of him—out of Anna's view—at Parker. "Mind your own fucking business."

She tries to wiggle free.

His fingernails dig into her scalp and clamp the strands of hair.

Footsteps—Parker's footsteps—back away from them.

No.

An engine starts in the parking lot.

No. Anna wiggles again. *He's not leaving.*

Her assailant yanks her head back up, pressing the blade to her neck. The tip slides gently against her skin.

She watches as Parker backs out of the park, looks back at her, then peels off.

No. He fucking left me? What am I going to do? How can I get away? She tries to look around, but he tightens his grip. Her scalp burns. "I bet you have a small dick."

"What the fuck did you say to me?" He presses the knife's tip harder against her skin.

She feels the cut, the blood pooling into a drop at its seam.

"I'll show you how fucking big my cock is, bitch." He shoves her over the bench, cutting the back of her pants. The blade slices at her skin, cutting along her lower spine.

She swings all her weight to the right. His fingers twist in her hair—yanking her back up. She swings left. He stumbles back, and his grip loosens. She twists, kicking him to the ground. His fingers tighten in her hair, pulling her closer—down toward him. He swings the knife and yanks Anna closer until her roots bleed. She jerks back one last time. The hair tears from its follicles. She falls on her ass. Mud smears into the cut down her back. She rolls and runs as fast as she can, not caring where to go.

His yells follow her into the fog.

She can't see more than three feet in front of her, but keeps running, hoping somewhere in her brain is the layout of the park, mapped out. *Right*. She pivots and makes for the playground. Sure enough, it is 10 steps in front of her. She can hide in the covered slide. She jumps up on the structure and the metal clanks, giving away her location. *Crap.* She hops down, falling on her hands in the wood chips.

He comes into the ring of visibility.

She pushes off the ground and sprints through the swings, toward the street. She takes a right, down an alley, and a left past a row of townhouses. The park disappears behind her. In lost breath, she rounds the next building, and stops, leaning against its brick wall. Her heart pounds. *Oh my God.* It pounds so loud she can't hear if he's coming, or how close he is. She peeks around the corner.

Headlights come at her.

She draws back, presses her back up against the side of the building again, and stares out onto the street.

A small hatchback car putts by.

She rests her head against the brick and breathes in the thick fog.

HIDDEN

ANNA WANTS TO GO HOME, BUT KELLEY'S PLACE IS closer—within walking distance, and she could use a beer. Kelley's townhouse is across from the school campus, not far from the café. Her Audi is stowed in the garage and a large blowup ghost sways in its place in the driveway. Orange lights hang around every window, stretching two stories above the garage. Pop music, some bullshit song about girls shaking their asses, spills out the front door onto the small lawn.

One drink, then home.

Anna starts up the stairs for the door. A slutty fairy with red hair storms out, yelling back over her shoulder, "I didn't mean for this to happen..."

Mr. Perfect-smile, Dominic, comes running out after her in Superman tights.

You've got to be kidding. Two drinks. Anna glances back at the spandex hugging his groin. *Or more.*

"Babe, it's not ..." He glances at Anna, doing a double take, continuing down the steps after the slutty fairy. "It's not our fault —"

She stops, looks him in the face, and yells, "She tried to kill herself! Don't you care?"

He stands there as she walks off.

Anna hurries inside, away from him, looking for a freakin' beer. The foyer is a sea of people, costumes, and faceless creatures pretending to resemble anything human. Anna draws up her hoodie and pulls at the edges of her sleeves, trying to bury herself deeper in it. A group of witches snicker at her from the corner.

Screw 'em. She squeezes between a robot and a blowup-penis, heading for the kitchen. It is brighter there, with fewer people all congregated around the counter.

A girl wearing the same pants as Anna—Kelley's pants— leans against the counter as Anna opens the refrigerator. "What are you supposed to be? Some pathetic piece of white trailer-trash?" She steps closer and slides her finger along the cut in Anna's back. "A whore?"

71

It burns. Anna wants to tell her to fuck off, but she feels bad for her. *I would rather be myself than anything like her.* But that isn't true. She would give anything to be someone else right now.

The fridge is pretty cleaned out, except a pack of cheap beer and a bottle of wine. She takes the wine and grabs a beer, nudging the door closed with her hip. Her hoodie brushes against the girl's slutty medieval dress. Anna shoves her lips against the girls, making her feel that she is real—that she is a person of flesh and blood too. She pulls away and exits the kitchen, bumping right into Kelley.

Kelley's costume is amazing. She looks like Zuul from the original Ghostbusters, down to red eyes that almost glow. She smiles. "Hey!"

"What the fuck was that?" Medieval Bitch yells, storming up behind Anna. "You little slut."

Kelley barricades the attack, glancing back at Anna. Her eyes stop on Anna's cheek—at the bruise that feels like it will explode. "Jesus, Anna."

I'm not doing this. Anna looks at the crowd of people: people she has waited on, people who remind her that she doesn't belong there. *They want to see my pain? I can show them my pain.* Her fists ball and she screams over Kelley's shoulder, "Oh, I'm sorry I thought you said you like whores."

Kelley crosses her arms.

Anna's supposed to shut up, be a polite guest, let them say whatever the fuck they want to her, about her. Why not? She's just the friend who makes Kelley feel better about herself. "You want to know what I am?" Anna looks at Kelley. She feels sorry for her. Kelley has to put on a front, conform to be just like them, hide who she really wants to be. "I'm the girl you will never be."

Kelley uncrosses her arms.

"Happy Halloween," Anna says, holding out the wine and pushing past the crowd now watching them. She makes it to the front door. Cold air pushes against her as she steps outside.

The inflatable ghost waves from the driveway.

Happy Halloween.

Dominic stands in her path, talking to a group of guys. Anna really doesn't want to see him.

Tires squeal in the distance. Conversations out on the lawn stop. Everyone's eyes move to the road. Headlights come sailing around the corner—it is three black Hummers.

Anna's heart jumps. If she takes off down the road, they will easily take her out.

Another two Hummers approach from the opposite direction, tearing into the driveway, flattening the ghost.

Anna shoves her way back into the house, through the crowd.

"Cops!" someone yells.

"You dipshit," another says. "They aren't cops ... it says Meadowlark. Wait. What's Meadowlark?"

A girl says, "Google it, shit-head."

Anna takes a set of stairs that are squished between the living room and kitchen. The door at the top is closed. She tries its doorknob. It is locked. The murmur below grows louder. She rams her shoulder into the door. *Ouch.* She loses her balance and totters on the top step. She hunches down and rams the door again. It swings open and momentum carries her into the room, falling face first. Her cheek scrapes against the rug, urging a bruise to surface.

A guy—the surfer guy from the van—stands over her with his hand held out. He is dressed in a tight, white 1970s suit.

The lines of a bed behind him come into focus. It is a bedroom. *Oh, my God, he's up here with a girl and I just came busting in….* Anna ignores his hand and sits up, reaching for the wine bottle and beer can she has dropped.

Five people sit half-circle on the bed. Three females: a gypsy, a cat, and a nun. Two males: a cowboy and she doesn't even know what—a homemade something.

Downstairs goes quiet.

Gypsy-girl jumps off the bed and runs to the window. "Oh, man, look at this…"

They all crowd around.

"Isn't that … you know, that guy whose girlfriend tried to kill herself?" says the nun.

Anna glances around the room. *I need to hide.*

"What's Meadowlark?" says the cowboy.

The bed. Anna pulls up the bed skirt. It is too small to hide under. *Damn it.* She stands up. The top of her head whacks surfer boy's chin.

James bends over in pain, clenching his jaw.

"I'm so ... sorry." Anna goes to comfort him, but pulls back. *There's no time.* Those Meadowlark guys will be storming up the steps any minute. *The back windows.* She presses her face against the windowpane and looks down. It is too far to jump and the neighboring roof isn't close enough.

"What happened to you?" he says.

"Nothing." Anna slumps into a pile on the floor below the window and pops open the beer. It's no use. She is screwed. She puts the beer to her lips, chugs until it is empty, and throws it to the rug.

James' eyes follow it. "You know…"

"Oh, shit," says the cat, "they're dragging him away."

Anna wipes the beer from her lips. *Maybe they're not after me.* "So what the hell are you guys doing up here?" Anna twists the cork top to the wine. It doesn't budge. She pulls, twists, yanks, and chews on it. "Is this an orgy or something?"

James puts his hand on top of hers. He is wearing a huge, gaudy, plastic-gold ring on his thumb.

Anna starts to laugh and then cry.

He brushes the hoodie back and gasps.

The faces pressed to the window turn to face them. They too breathe hard enough to be heard.

"Anna…" he says.

How the hell did he remember my name?

He reaches to swipe the hair from her cheek, hesitates, and pulls back. "What happened to you?"

She pulls the hoodie up again and leans her head back

against the wall. *What am I supposed to tell him? That I was meeting a much older guy in the park to screw?* Anna shakes her head. *No.*

The crowd of eyes return to the window. Then everyone scatters like cockroaches, clinging to the wall, out of view from the lawn.

"Shit," says the cowboy. "They saw us."

"They're coming," says Cat.

"Ladies and gentlemen," a deep, male voice bellows out from downstairs.

"You can't let them find me," says Anna.

James is still trying to work his brain around Anna's torn hair and bruised face—she can see it. The wonder of how the naked girl from earlier managed to mess herself up even more than before.

"Please," she says.

His eyes snap from their trance and search the room. "The closet."

No way. That's the first place they'll look.

"Alice, shut the door," James says. The Gypsy does so. James opens the closet. Inside is a mess: piles of wrinkled clothes on the floor, blouses half-hung on hangers, mismatched shoes piled on the floor. The top shelf is filled with folded blankets and a stack of sun hats. James throws them to the floor, interlaces his hands and holds them out like Anna needs a boost. "Okay, get up there."*What?*

Footsteps stamped up the stairs.

Anna shoves her foot in his palm and climbs up, squeezing onto the top shelf.

He jams the blankets over and around her, then shuts the closet door.

All the air is sucked into the fabric surrounding Anna. The pocket her arms have created around her mouth grows thick with carbon dioxide.

The footsteps up the stairs fall faint all at once, and then stop. A fist pounds against the door. Muffled voices follow. The agents break down the door and start yelling, pissed that the door was locked, and of their blatant insubordination.

"Check the girls," one says.

The women make a squealing noise.

The closet door bangs open.

Anna holds her breath. Seconds feel like hours. Her lungs burn.

"Check the bed," says one.

"She's not here," says another.

The closest agent punches his fist into the closet door.

Anna closes her eyes, picturing the unopened wine bottle laying on the bedroom floor. *I should've drunk all that.* She can't hold her breath much longer.

"Let's go," says the guy, yanking his fist from the door.

Footsteps descend the stairway.

Anna gasps, pulling the air through the tight cotton fibers of the blankets. Her heart pounds more quickly—louder in her chest than before. She closes her eyes, hoping she won't die.

Take Me Home

JAMES UNPACKS THE BLANKETS AS THE MEADOWLARK agents take off.

Anna's lungs swell with air.

James rolls her into his arms and lays her on the floor, leaning over her. "You okay?"

She lays there, looking up past him, at the ceiling.

The crowd downstairs murmurs.

"Hey," one of the girls says. "We're heading over to Alice's. You coming with?"

"I'll catch up," says James. He leans back, out of view.

Anna lets her body sink into the rug as her lungs pound back to normal.

The group descends the stairs.

James leans back into view, brushing a lock of Anna's hair from her bruised cheek.

She flinches.

His fingers move abruptly and he whispers, "Sorry."

Downstairs quiets.

Footsteps pound up the steps and a gasp comes from a woman as she reaches the top. Kelley's voice shakes as she says, "Shit."

"Yeah," says James. "They kicked it in."

"My parents are gonna be pissed," she says.

"Don't sweat it," says James. "I can put in a new one."

She sinks down beside Anna, smearing the makeup on her cheeks. "I can't believe they took Dominic."

"He's a dick, anyway," slips out of Anna's mouth.

"Anna," says Kelley in reprimand.

Anna sits up, tugging the hoodie tight. "Well, he is."

James stares at Anna, waiting for more of an explanation.

She crosses her arms, trying to shake the feeling that she is sitting in James's van naked all over again. She wants to go home, but those agents could be headed to Mom's. *Where else … where else can I go?* If she knew where her dad was, she could stay with him. But she doesn't give a crap where he is. She brushes the hair from her cheek, scraping the bruise swelling beneath her skin. *The bar. No. It'll be packed.* The park flashes into her thoughts. She tightens her hoodie, drawing the cotton down like a blizzard is coming. Nausea floods her throat. She searches for the wine bottle. It's behind her, still beneath the window with the damn cork stuck in it. *Great.* She leans back and grabs it.

"Hey," James says, resting a hand on her knee. "You want a ride home?"

Why can't he be offering a freakin' corkscrew? Instead he is offering her a ride—always offering rides. She doesn't want a ride. She wants to drink the bottle of wine and drown out the fact that her scalp is bleeding, that chunks of her hair are missing, and her face is beaten. All she wants is for the night to bleed into dawn. Maybe tomorrow will be different. Maybe she will wake up from this horrible dream.

He looks down at the bottle and pulls a keyring from his pocket. Hanging among the clutter is a nine-inch screw. He grins, holds it up, and extends a hand for the bottle.

You've got to be kidding. Anna can't hold back the smile puckering beneath her lips. She hands him the bottle. He removes the cork and hands the wine back to her. She should offer him some, but instead places the bottle to her lips so quickly it bangs against her front tooth. She downs it anyway. It's nasty, but nothing compares to the colon cleanse she forced down yesterday.

James makes a concerned huff and puff and then begins to chuckle. "Damn. I think you better…"

Anna tilts her head back enough to consume the last drops. The hood of her sweatshirt slides down.

Kelley's voice comes like a freight train out of nowhere, "What the hell happened to you?"

Anna can feel the cold air fill the spaces of her missing hair.

"Oh my God, Anna," Kelly's voice lowers, carrying a hint of reverence Anna has never heard before.

James leans closer, reaching his hand out like he is going to comfort her, then pulls back.

She doesn't need his comfort. The wine seeps into her stomach, warming her body. The room spins and she plants her hands on the rug, grounding herself.

"Jesus," says Kelley. "Would you drive her home?"

James rests his hand on Anna's shoulder.

"No." Anna pulls back. "They know where I live … If I go home they'll…" The image of those Meadowlark guys storming into her house and tying up Mom and Jeremy—duct-taping their mouths, dragging their lifeless bodies from the trailer and throwing them into the back of a Hummer—is too much to bear. Then she gives in. "Take me home."

UNCOVERED

RAIN PELTS THE ROOF AND BANGS AGAINST THE windows. Anna rolls over. Mom is tucked under the covers beside her, reeking of alcohol, like usual. Anna turns her eyes to the rain running down the windowpane. It is going to be a long winter. Her head is killing her.

Her mom rolls, pulling the covers off her head. It isn't Mom. It is James.

What the hell? Anna can't remember anything after leaving Kelley's last night. *What am I wearing?* Images of the meth-head pulling the knife from his pants swells in her thoughts. *I can't remember...* She lifts the comforter—still in her hoodie and pants. *Was it real?* She feels for the cut down her spine from having her pants sliced from her. *Was that how I spent Halloween?* The tips of her fingers scrape against dry blood. Pain confirms reality.

"Hey," says James.

What is it with all these "heys" all the time? *Wait. Is he wearing clothes?* Anna yanks the cover away from him.

He smiles. "Looking for something?"

Okay. He is wearing clothes. Her head pounds. *Damn.*

The bedroom door bursts open and ricochets off the wall. Mom stands in the doorway. "Hey..." She notices James and her eyes widen.

Anna jumps out of bed and blocks Mom's view of him. "It's not what it—"

"Jeremy!" Mom yells back into the kitchen.

Crap. The rule has always been: no guys. Period. Not here in her pristine trailer.

Mom's eyes shoot back at Anna like darts.

Jeremy steps into view beside her, holding a cupcake piled high with extra icing. He glances at Anna but is 95 percent more focused on the cupcake. "What?"

Mom waves him further in so he can see James.

Can we get this over with?

Jeremy peels off the cupcake wrapper and stuffs half the thing in his mouth.

Dad—Russell—aka the piece of crap sperm donor and deserter—would have flown off the handle the instant James came into view. Sometimes Anna swears Russell cares more about her precious cherry being popped than he actually cares about her. *Where was he last night when I needed him?*

Jeremy finishes off the cupcake, licks the icing from his fingers, and wipes his mouth with the bottom of his wife-beater. Then he walks away.

He walked away. No yelling, no comment, no reprimand, no dragging the guy out of my bed and out the front door.

"We'll talk about this later," says Mom. She backs out the door, pulling it shut behind her.

Anna flops down onto the bed. *I don't understand.*

James sits up and scoots closer from behind. "I told them everything."

"What?" *How could he? It wasn't his place. Who the hell does he think he is? Coming into my life...* She spins around to yell at him. His lips are right there—an inch from hers. She wants to lean into them, reward him for driving her home last night, and then... She can't remember anything after that.

His fingers brush her cheek above the bruise. "Your mom wants to know what happened to your..." He draws his hand away.

My hair? Anna stands up and walks over to the full-length mirror hanging on the bedroom door. Large clumps of hair are gone from her scalp. Scabs of blood mask the chunks of flesh missing. *Oh, my...* A warm tear drains out of the corner of her eye. The side of her face is a dark purple. She twists, trying to see the gash along her spine.

James gets up and comes over, gently nudging her chin toward his.

She closes her eyes and turns away.

"Hey..." he says.

"Why are you still here?" She glances back at the mirror. Her pale skeleton stares back. The bruise on her face darkens the bags beneath her eyes. *Who am I kidding?* She lets her eyes judge her. The image cuts deeper into the regret of her past decisions. She has been so stupid. *Who would meet a guy in the park? I should've screwed him in the car, then none of this would've happened.* She opens her eyes.

James sits back on the bed.

She must look like a worn out whore. Thrown around and beaten like she is just some hole to stick it in, no rights to her own decisions, no voice worth listening to. The heater vent kicks on, stirring the cold air.

Concealing any emotion, James' eyes follow the edge of Anna's shirt to her hips.

Anna jerks her zipper down and tears off her pants. "Is this what you want?"

His lips part. His chest lifts with a breath.

"Is this what you came for?" she asks.

He should crave her so bad that he must wrap her into his arms and force himself upon her. But he doesn't. He folds his hands in his lap and closes his lips.

She feels so gross. *Why would he want this?* She is so thin, too flat-chested. "You think I should suck you off for a ride?"

He just sits there staring at her chest, unmoving. He begins, "You—"

There is a knock at the door.

"In a minute!" Anna scoops a pair of jeans off the floor, sliding them on, and grabs a bra hanging on the doorknob. She looks over at James, and then drops it. *Why the hell doesn't he want me?* She rummages through a dresser drawer, searching through the sea of black, oversized band tee-shirts and grabs the tightest, brightest shirt she has—a vintage-green shirt from the Oregon Country Fair.

Typically Anna doesn't have enough money to do anything after she buys a ticket. But this year a guy's girlfriend was screaming at him outside the entrance—something about him staring at one of the topless-painted girls that walked by. He started waving her ticket in the air, yelling, "Who wants a free ticket?"

Silence exploded like a nuclear bomb.

"Free ticket," he said, looking back at his girl. "Any topless woman want a free ticket?"

She cursed him under her breath and walked away.

Anna wasn't passing up a free ticket. So she walked over to claim it. "I'll take it."

He offered it out, but he didn't look at her. He was too busy watching his woman walk away.

Kelley came running up, asking, "What are you doing?"

Anna thanked the guy and wished him luck, then made for the fair entrance.

"Why did you do that?" she nagged.

Anna isn't like her. She can't afford everything she wants. She has to scrape and save for months. It took Kelley one phone call to her parents and—bam—she has anything she wants.

Anna yanks the shirt from the bedroom drawer. The screen-printed tree on the front is still as vibrant as the day Anna bought it. Its roots flow into a circle surrounding it, protecting it. Kelley bought some pink star design that is completely faded now. *She's got so much more than me.* Maybe if Anna was more like Kelley, she could get out of this piece of shit life. *Shit, my head hurts. I'm so sick of being me.*

James approaches from behind Anna, his chest presses lightly against her back. She takes a step away from him and pulls the shirt on, searching the pile of makeup atop the dresser. *If I layer on the eyeliner and foundation, maybe I can hide the bruise.* Red lipstick will dull the puffy corner of her lip. *My hair —torn and ripped.* Anna has a hat, a beanie woven with yarn, somewhere. *Where is it?*

Another knock comes at the door, louder than before.

James moves away and answers it.

Mom peeks around the door. "Are you going to work today?"

Crap. She'll see my hair and start asking questions. Where is that hat? There it is, beside the bed on the floor. Anna grabs it and tugs it on, glancing at the clock. *Crap.* Anna is late for work. *Great. This day is getting better and better.*

Mom's eyes narrow and she steps into the room. "What's going on with you?"

"Nothing," says Anna.

"Don't give me that shit." Mom takes another step closer.

James moves back, granting full access to Anna's room.

Anna cuts her off.

"Only ...," Mom says.

"Mom," Anna says. Mom wants answers and Anna has none. Anna doesn't even know what had happened: at Kelley's, Brenda's next door, or the medical clinic. *The medical clinic.* "Did they ever say what happened at the clinic?"

Worry fills Mom's face. "What do you mean? Did this happen at the—"

"No." Anna looks at James for some help, but he just stands there. "What about that thing last night at Kelley's? Was that on the news?"

His lips clamp shut.

"I'm not crazy..." Anna slumps onto the bed. A chill creeps up her spine, igniting the feeling that the guy from last night is still there, like his breath against her neck as the cold blade of his knife pressed against her skin. "Some guy..."

They both freeze, staring at Anna.

"He ... he tried to ... he..." She looks up at her mother.

Mom's lips draw into a frown. She bows her head, backing out of the room, closing the door.

"You want a ride?" asks James.

MEADOWLARK

ANNA THROWS ON HER SNEAKERS AND STORMS INTO THE
kitchen. James follows. Jeremy and Mom are hiding in her
bedroom. A leaning cupcake falls from the pile on the counter.
An unopened envelope—junk mail—is folded in half so it will
stand up in front of the pile. Mom's handwriting reads: *You're
my Only.*

Part of Anna wishes Jeremy was her dad, her birth dad.
Instead, she knows she is genetically half-asshole.

James picks up the fallen cupcake. Icing smears down his
finger. He sets the cupcake down, wiping the extra icing off on a
hand towel.

A car door slams shut outside, in the direction of Megan's trailer.

Anna looks out through the kitchen window. A black Meadowlark Hummer sits in Megan's driveway. Anna ducks down.

"What?" asks James. He looks out the window and then joins her, cowering behind the counter.

Anna hurries to the front door, clearing any view from the kitchen window—spreading the window blind of her trailer door.

Two female agents hop out. Anna spreads the blinds a little more. The glass fogs beneath her lips. The driver has a tight ponytail that swings as she approaches Megan's neighboring trailer. The other agent is more butch-military grade. She glances back at Anna's trailer door.

Crap. Anna can get away if the agents go inside Megan's place. Anna looks down her own trailer, to her bedroom—to the windows much too high to escape out of. There is no way out other than through the front door. A breath forces itself though Anna's lips, blowing dust off the blinds. The blinds bang against the door with her breath. *Crap.* Anna angles them down and looks back at James. "What do we do?"

He looks away, to her thin tee-shirt.

What the hell is wrong with men? She peeks round the side of the blind.

The agents knock on Megan's trailer.

The door flings open. Hector appears. A cigarette flops between his lips as words spill from them, "What do you want? We're not interested in your bible—"

Ms. Ponytail-agent shoves a badge in his face.

Hector's cigarette falls from his lips—onto the deck—and rolls, stopping at the agent's boot.

"Does Megan Lansworth live here?" Ponytail digs her heel into the smoldering tobacco, smudging it into the wood.

Hector yells back over his shoulder, "Meg!"

The chunky slut replaces him in the doorway. The color washes from her cheeks.

"My name is Agent Glenn," Ms. Ponytail says. "This," she motions back to the other, "is Agent Sam. We'd like to ask you a few questions."

Megan pops a piece of gum.

Agent Sam takes something out from her front pocket and holds it out to Megan. "Have you ever seen this girl?"

Megan glances at Anna's trailer, popping a bubble. "Nope."

Agent Glenn's hand fists at her side. "Have you been having intercourse with a..." she scrolls over a screen on her wristwatch, "Dominic Gambini?"

Megan's neck almost snaps, looking back into her trailer. She squeezes out onto the porch, forcing the agents back, and yanks the door closed behind her. The conversation turns to whispers.

The agents simultaneously look over and flee Megan's porch for Anna's front door.

She thinks I ratted her out. Crap. Anna glances around the room. *Crap.* She can hide, but she has a hunch that won't work.

They knock at the door.

The house phone rings.

Oh my God.

The knock morphs into something louder. Agent Glenn raises her voice, "We know you're in there."

The phone continues to ring.

Mom runs out from the bedroom and reaches for the phone hanging on the kitchen wall. She catches sight of us, smiles, and withdraws her hand. Her shoulders droop and Anna knows it is in relief that she is still home.

The next knock shakes the trailer door. "Open up. Last shot."

Mom's eyes widen with a what-the-heck-is-that look.

James holds up his hand, instructing her to stay put.

The pounding comes again, and then whispers—a plot to break down the door.

James nudges Anna behind him and opens the door. "Hey, man," he stretches his arms to the ceiling and yawns, "we're trying to sleep in here."

Agent Glenn's eyes meet Anna's. Anna longs to look away, but only a coward would do that, and she is losing her patience with being pathetic.

"Do you live … here?" Agent Sam shoves a Homeland Security badge out, stopping short as her eyes connect to James'. The nose stud in her left nostril twinkles as her weight shifts and the words fade.

James clears his throat.

Glenn tilts her head, attempting to look deeper into the trailer. "Can I see some ID?"

"No," says James.

Oh, my God, he's going to get us killed.

Sam's cheeks blush a little.

Glenn's fingers reach for her holster. "Where are your parents?"

James grabs Anna's waist, pulling her close to him. "Just two love birds here."

Glenn's eyes narrow. "Looks more like a punching bag to me."

James grins and takes a step closer to the women, biting his lip. "You wanna feel it?"

"Excuse me," Glenn says.

What is he doing? Anna heads toward Mom, who is now gone. Mom knows when to flee.

"Wait, babe, I didn't mean that ..." James yells back to Anna over his shoulder, and slams the trailer door in the agents' faces.

Oh my God—

He catches up to Anna, chewing on the bottom of his lip, and takes a breath, smiling.

The two agents mumble outside the door in argument, head back to the Hummer, and take off down the road.

GRAVITY

ANNA HOPS ONTO THE CITY BUS.

James' hippie van sails past the window. Anna can't accept
another ride from him. He is too clean-cut—too nice, even for a
dirty surfer.

The dragonfly tattoo's reflection flows over passing cars,
invisible to them. Ms. Tumult is sweet, but madly obsessed
about punctuality. If this is the 10 o'clock bus, then Anna is two
hours late. She knew the phone call Mom attempted to answer—
the phone call that pierced the air while those agents stood on
her doorstep at the worst possible time—was Ms. Tumult.

Anna's mind replays the incident in her bedroom that

morning. She shouldn't have been so short with James. He hadn't been anything but helpful, but she felt worthless around him.

The bus stops and a middle-aged woman climbs aboard, dragging a young girl behind her. The girl stops in the aisle and stares long and hard at Anna. Her mother stares at the cell phone in her hand while taking a seat and yanking the girl in behind her.

The girl peeks around the seat, down the aisle.

Anna feels for the beanie, making sure it covers the horror and damage of her poor choices. It is still there. She sinks into the seat, resting her head against the window. The dragonfly continues its dance in the world caught between reflection and reality.

The bus sails on, until greeting the same sidewalk—the same stop—Anna takes every day. She navigates the aisle, passing the mother and child.

"What happened to you?" says the girl, grabbing onto Anna's fingers as she passes.

"Gravity!" says her mother, yanking her closer, away from Anna, not bothering to lift her eyes away from the phone.

The girl's little fingers pull away.

Anna should keep walking, but she stops and kneels down beside the girl's seat. There are so many stories, so many lessons Anna wants to share. She would start with making sure the girl realizes—that she knows—there are bad people in the world, ones who will take what they want, rape what they want, and are so wounded that they cannot feel another's pain. She wants to make sure the girl is scared enough to be safe.

Gravity's big brown eyes scan the bruise and puffy lip concealed beneath a sheet of makeup.

Instead, unsure why or from where the words manifest, Anna says, "I survived."

"Gravity," her mother's voice raises, but she still doesn't lift her eyes away from her phone.

The bus doors begin to swing shut.

Anna leans closer to those brown eyes and whispers, "You'll survive too."

The girl's eyes light up.

Anna stands and runs for the door with her hands flying. "Wait!"

The driver's eyes narrow in the rearview mirror and he reopens the doors.

She jumps out and turns around, watching the bus leave. A chill pushes up her spine. The fog from last night has lifted, but a weight hangs in her heart.

The little girl named Gravity presses her face up against the window, giving a slow wave before she disappears.

A two-foot-tall owl is perched in a tree across the street. Its talons dig into the branch. Its deep grey feathers ruffle with the wind.

A gust tugs at Anna's beanie. She pulls it down and heads for the café.

The owl's large yellow eyes follow.

She glances back before grabbing hold of the café doorknob.

The owl's neck cranks completely in her direction.

Anna's heart jerks and she yanks open the door.

Conversations pour out onto the sidewalk.

The owl screeches.

Anna's heart jumps.

The bell above the door jingles, bringing her back to reality —to a world where no one looks up to greet her.

Ms. Tumult is behind the register. Her face is red from over exertion.

Anna weaves through the line of customers.

Beads of sweat drip along Ms. Tumult's hairline. Her eyes light up when she sees Anna. "Where have you been?"

Ms. Tumult loses concentration, realizing Anna's shirt is much too thin for the autumn day.

Anna crosses her arms. *I should've worn a bra.*

"Never mind." Ms. Tumult nods toward the café aprons hanging beside the espresso machine.

Anna throws one on and joins Ms. Tumult, grabbing order slips, compressing beans, swirling syrup, and steaming milk. An hour easily passes before the customer line shrinks to two black coffees.

Ms. Tumult wipes her brow and leans on the counter. "Two twelve-ounce coffees!" She nods toward the prep area. "Can you check on Kelley?"

"Kelley's here?" Anna stands up, looking over Ms. Tumult's shoulder into the back.

"Make sure she's not still in the powder room. She ran off right before you got here, complaining her stomach hurt." Ms. Tumult forbids any other synonym for needing to use the restroom, especially in the customer-centered areas.

Anna steps into the back. The bathroom door is shut. It wouldn't be the first time Kelley hid during a huge rush of people. Anna taps on the door. "Kelley? You in there? You okay?"

There is no answer.

Anna knocks, then leans her ear against the door. "Kelley?" All Anna can hear is her heartbeat radiating off the wood. The pounding increases. She tries the doorknob. It turns. She nudges the door open, giving Kelley ample time to compose herself. "Kelley?"

Kelley sits on the floor, hunched in the corner beside the sink, shivering. Her hair is wet, hiding her face.

"Kelley." Anna plops down beside her, wiping the hair from her face.

Kelley's eyes roll into the back of her head. Sweat drips from her pores.

Crap. All the visions of the medical center flood Anna's thoughts. She springs to her feet, runs through the food-prep area, and rounds the espresso machine to the front counter.

Ms. Tumult is taking an order over the phone, with her back to her.

Anna grabs the phone from her hand and hangs up.

"What are you—" says Ms. Tumult.

"She needs a doctor," says Anna.

Ms. Tumult's eyes roll as the gears in her head try to wrap themselves around Anna's words. She glances over the crowd, making sure no one has overheard, then grabs Anna's arm and drags her into the back prep-area. "Now listen ..."

"Suzanne ..." Anna stares at the cracked bathroom door. She shouldn't have used Ms. Tumult's name. Mom told her to keep it professional, no matter what. But she had, and it has gotten her attention.

"Well," Ms. Tumult holds her tongue and glances at the bathroom door "let's see."

Anna hurries to the back bathroom, slides her fingers into the crack of the door and pushes it open. It is empty. *How?* She steps inside, making sure Kelley isn't hiding behind the bathroom door.

"She probably went home," Ms. Tumult says from the doorway.

The café phone rings and she hurries back to the front room.

But... Anna looks over the small prep area, left then right. There is no one. *What's wrong with me? There's no way Kelley could've moved—not in the state she's in. There's no way I'm seeing things.* Anna returns to the front to Ms. Tumult. The café is extremely loud.

Ms. Tumult hands Anna an order, following her gaze over the packed seats. "Isn't this great?"

Anna has never seen it so busy before—bustling at the seams. "Why—?"

"Apparently classes were cancelled for today. Some preparedness drill, earthquake—something." She shovels coffee grinds into a coffee maker and starts it. "You hear about the bear attack at Yosemite?"

"The National Park?" asks Anna.

"Yeah. Late last night. And then another this morning."

"What about the thing at the medical center?" says Anna. *What kind of drugs had they given me?*

"What medical center?" She pulls a blue can from the shelf (her good-quality coffee stash), pops it open and grabs a spoonful.

"The one here in town," says Anna.

"Here?" She freezes, letting the spoon sink into the coffee grinds.

Anna shouldn't have said anything. She steps closer to Ms. Tumult to comfort her, but she doesn't know how. The café is so damn loud. She leans into Ms. Tumult's ear, "Some guy killed people."

"What people?"

"A doctor, an intern, the security guard."

Ms. Tumult's face says it all, she doesn't believe her.

"Then there were these two guys yesterday, then at Kelley's last night ... Then at my next door neighbors' house..."

Ms. Tumult touches Anna's bruised cheek. A sharp pain shoots through the tender nerves. Concealer makeup smears onto her thumb. She pulls her hand away, rubbing the foundation between her fingers.

"Now," Anna says, "the café's packed. Because of some bull shit story about emergency preparedness."

"I'm sorry," says Ms. Tumult.

What?

"I was so busy with them"—she slides her fingers across Anna's puffy lip—"that I didn't notice."

Ouch. Anna pulls back.

"Go home." Ms. Tumult nods at Anna, forcing a smile. "I'll even pay you for the day." She looks out at the crowd. "I think I can afford it."

Anna crosses her arms, waiting for Ms. Tumult to change her mind.

Beads of sweat collect on Ms. Tumult's forehead. A drop rolls away from her hairline.

"How about I stay?" says Anna. "I'll just take it slow."

Ms. Tumult smiles and nods, leaning her lips against Anna's forehead, kissing it, then pulls away, brushing the knitted beanie. "What's with the hat?"

A man clears his throat from the other side of the counter.

Anna's heartbeat spikes. She spins around, blubbering, "What would you like?"

It is James. He simpers, no doubt finding amusement where there shouldn't be any. "I'll take a spinach quiche and an oolong tea."

"Is that it?" Anna says, glancing back over her shoulder.

Ms. Tumult is staring at them, unaware that she has spilled the spoonful of coffee grounds all over the counter.

"That's it." He slides a $20 bill across the counter and walks away.

"Do you know him?" Ms. Tumult stands at the register, waiting for the money.

"Sort of." Anna hands it over.

Ms. Tumult punches the order into the register.

Anna spins the quiche dish, stopping on the largest piece, scoops it out, and nukes it.

The register pops open. Ms. Tumult pulls $10.75 in change out. "He's cute. And he tips well." She offers the change to Anna. "Go ahead. You keep it. Put it in your pocket."

The microwave pings.

Anna takes the money and arranges the serving tray, looking for the table he chose. It is smack in the middle of the café, one of the more unpopular sections. There, tables have chairs instead of booths. Anna weaves between people, ignoring the fact that they can see through the layer of foundation—see her front and center—exposed—prey for their judgment. She sets the tray down across from him, unloading it.

"Well," he says, "that's some service."

Anna gives him a smile for that one. But she cannot keep a $10 tip. It is too much. And she doesn't want to be one of those girls that can be bought. She digs into her pocket, pulls out the change, and sets it on the table. People start to stare, so she sits down. "I owe you some gas money."

He stiffens in his seat. His smile disappears. Her gesture did something—something he never dealt with before. He picks up his fork slowly and slices a piece of quiche off, shoving it into his mouth.

A cell phone rings.

He drops the fork, leans to one side, and pulls a phone from his back pocket.

It is perfect timing. Anna heads back to the counter, getting out of taking his charity money.

"Anna!" he says, running up behind her. "There's a fire. I've got to go."

"What?"

He moves the food tray to one side, pulling Anna into his other arm, and pressing his lips against hers—slow and hard. He pulls away to whisper, "Can we talk later?"

With him so close—his chest pressing against hers, and the fact that she is completely and totally vulnerable—she kisses him back. "Yes."

He lets go, hands her the tray, and heads for the door.

Wait. What did he just say? A fire. What fire? She is going to scream her questions across the café, but he has already gone, leaving the bell jingling alone. She turns around to the counter.

Ms. Tumult stares at her from the espresso machine.

Anna can't hide the grin plastered all over her face. She empties the tray and there sits the $10.75 in change.

Night Walkers

The noon rush has come and gone. Stillness envelops the café. The wind picks up outside. Red maple leaves blow across the street and stick to the Eiffel Tower etched into the front window.

Ms. Tumult left with a friend after the rush depleted. Now, two hours later, she is crossing the street out front. The bell jingles, announcing her entrance as she fights with the wind to pull the door shut behind her.

A cold breeze squeezes in, whipping through the café, digging down into Anna's bones.

Ms. Tumult huffs, leaning against the door, "Did I miss anything?"

"Five mochas and a chai latte," says Anna.

Ms. Tumult smirks, unravels a bright orange scarf from her neck and hangs it among the aprons. "Mara was telling me the medical center caught fire. That must be where your friend went."

What the hell would he be doing at a fire?

"Now the whole damn medical center is burning to the ground." She rubs her hands together trying to warm them. "Let's start cleaning up. Ben's Beans is on that side of town and the whole damn city is over there now."

Ben is her biggest competitor. Slowly but surely he is running her out of business. Probably because he offers punch cards—something she refuses to do.

"What about the late night rush?" says Anna.

Ms. Tumult shivers as if the wind has found a way in, exploding all around her. "I think tonight"—she grabs the scarf and wipes the foundation off Anna's cheek—"tonight we count our blessings." She looks at the scarf—the streaks of makeup. "Put the cheesecake that's in the fridge in the freezer. Then we'll put the displays in the back refrigerator for tonight. Got it?"

Anna nods and heads to the back. The prep area is a mess. Coffee grounds cover a table, empty milk cartons overflow beside the backdoor. The only item that didn't move today was the cheesecake. Ms. Tumult always prices it too high, almost six bucks for a slice—crazy. Anna opens the refrigerator and pulls the cheesecake to the shelf's edge, sliding it onto her arm. *Damn, it's cold.*

A large, dark object beside the backdoor catches Anna's attention. Her heart jerks. The cake wobbles in her arms. She leans back, peeking around the refrigerator door. It's only Ms. Tumult's black suede jacket hung over the broom. *Shit.* Anna laughs, steadying the cake. It's nothing but her stupid imagination playing tricks on her.

The hospital's burning. The intern's drooling mouth and crusty eyes flash through Anna's thoughts. *It's nothing.* She bumps the refrigerator door shut with her hip and heads for the freezer, balancing the cake while yanking its door open. Cold air rolls out.

Pots and pans clank to the floor in the front room.

Anna's heart jerks.

Ms. Tumult's curses follow the pans.

Anna relaxes, kicking the freezer door shut and slides the cake onto the prep table, running to Ms. Tumult's aide.

The pans lay on the floor and Ms. Tumult stands frozen above them, staring at her cell phone.

A female newscaster takes up the screen, braving the wind and rain outside Portland International Airport. "Breaking News" flashes across the bottom. The following stream of words is too small to read.

Ms. Tumult's hand shakes as she turns up the volume.

"All flights have just been grounded by Homeland Security nationwide," the newscaster yells above the wind. "More on that later. Back to you, Peter!"

Ms. Tumult leans against the counter, flicking through websites, looking for more information.

While she's glued to her phone, Anna needs to keep busy. Her mind quickly starts to torture her with thoughts. There are too many coincidences—too much crazy shit happening. Anna switches off the coffee machines.

"Shit," says Ms. Tumult.

Anna has never heard her curse before, and the word stops her dead in her tracks.

Ms. Tumult stares at the phone. "Check the Wi-Fi."

Anna glances beneath the counter. All the lights on the router are lit up. Nothing has changed. "Everything looks good."

Ms. Tumult's thumb flicks over the phone screen. "Damn internet stopped."

What?

"I'll try my data." She stays quiet for a while, checking through apps and exiting out of windows.

Anna leans over beside her.

Server unavailable.

Ms. Tumult's eyes drift past Anna. "Just clean up the mess." She stares at the backroom. "We can restock tomorrow morning." She walks into the prep room, puts on her coat, and wraps the messy orange scarf around her neck. "I'll … see you tomorrow."

"Okay." *That's really weird.* Anna has given up asking questions or trying to make sense of anything. It has all been so messed up since she drank the colon cleanse. She is waiting to wake up.

Ms. Tumult pushes the backdoor open, stops, turns back to grab the cheesecake off the counter, and heads for her Mercedes in the rear parking lot. The wind makes several attempts to knock the cake from her grip, but she eventually makes it safely to the car.

Anna yanks the door shut and slides the lock. The warm sound of the engine hums outside and fades from the alleyway. Wind pounds against the building. Anna runs from the back of the café to the front to lock the door. No way she is getting stuck with a last-minute customer tonight.

The pieces of mirror from the mosaic dragonfly flicker with light as she sprints by.

An entangled couple stumbles along outside, approaching the front door.

Anna runs harder, grabs the "open" sign on the door and flips it, turning the lock.

They keep going.

That was close. She turns around, leaning her back against the door's glass. The café is a mess. *Shoot.*

Someone pounds on the door behind her. The glass vibrates against her back.

It is James … dressed like a firefighter.

What the—?

"You gonna let me in?" he asks. Wind gusts, pushing against his helmet, revealing his smashed dreadlocks beneath.

"All planes have been grounded," the newscaster's voice echoes in her thoughts. She unlocks the door, pulling the knob. The wind pushes it open, nearly toppling her.

James steps in, taking his helmet off.

Anna laughs. He looks like a stripper.

"What?" he says, smiling—probably knowing exactly what she's thinking.

"Nothing," she says, heading for the kitchen. "You forgot your change."

"Oh," he says following her, fully aware he had left it.

"So is this a joke?" she says.

"What do you mean?" he says.

She turns around to face him.

His smile has grown to a shitty grin. He has likely used this same getup before to win a girl over. He pulls off his jacket and throws it to the floor, rocking his hips like there is music playing.

Anna cracks up, laughing. Her brain hurts. She can't process how crazy things have become. The laughter eases to a smile she can't wipe off. She heads over to clean the espresso machine. "So you're a fireman?"

He scoops the helmet and jacket up, leans against the counter, blocking Anna in, and grabs a can of whipped cream. "I'm whatever you want me to be."

Oh, Jesus.

He presses the nozzle of the can and whipped cream spits out all over.

Oh, my God. Anna titters, never wanting anyone more than she wants him in that very moment. Her heart pounds, longing for him. The scrapes in her scalp, her bruised cheek, and the cut down her back throbs—reminding her how white trash she is. *Oh God, I'm doing it again.* She looks at the floor. *What are you doing? Look at your hair, you're so ugly.* She slides her hands into her apron pocket.

"Hey," he says, "what's wrong?"

She hates it when people ask her that. *Who wants to say that shit out loud? Tell him how ugly I feel.* She heads for the prep room.

"Anna…" He follows.

They always do when you don't want them to. *Why won't he let it go? Leave it alone?*

He grabs her elbow, spinning her towards him. She is so ready to push him away, keep him from destroying everything that's left of her. But momentum stripes away any choice, as their chests come together. His breath touches her lips. He smells like a fresh campfire. *God. He smells so good.*

"You've got some whipped cream on you," he says.

No I don't—

He points the canister at her face and presses the nozzle. Whipped cream sprays across her nose and clumps in her beanie.

She gasps. *I can't believe he—*

He grabs her chin, tilts her face, and licks it off her cheek.

A chill jerks through her body and she wiggles back,

laughing. She grabs the canister, turns it on him, and sprays. Cream shoots out and plops to the floor. *Crap. It's all out.*

He scoops her up, loses his footing, stumbles, and falls. She lands first. His weight follows, pushing out all the air from her lungs as his body falls on hers. He planks instantly, gazing into her eyes. He looks away from hers, to the beanie.

The beanie! She reaches for it. Her fingers slide over a patch of skin. *Where's the damn beanie?* Her wounds have to look even more disgusting up close.

He backs off and sits up beside her.

She joins him, looking for the beanie—hanging her head low. *Every moment, every moment is always fucked up. I can't have one goddamn—*

"Have you cleaned them?" he says.

"What?" She looks up.

His eyes are already waiting for hers. They shoot around the room. He sits up on his knees and jumps to his feet. "You have a first-aid kit here?"

"In the bathroom." Anna hitches a thumb behind her and he runs off toward it. *The bathroom. Kelley!* Anna jumps to her feet and grabs the phone. She had meant to call Kelley. The day flew by and she had been spinning until James got there. Stuffed behind the register is an employee list. Ms. Tumult keeps it there, because she doesn't want to clutter her phone with employee phone numbers. In reality, she doesn't add anyone's number into her phone, because she knows she would abuse the accessibility.

Anna dials Kelley's number. It rings through the phone and materializes into a buzzing noise in proximity to Anna. *Where's it coming from?* It's close. Something pink fills the space between the register and counter. Anna tries to slide it out with her finger with no success.

"Who..." James comes out of nowhere.

Jesus. Anna's heart jumps and her body follows.

"...Are you calling?" he asks, holding a bottle of peroxide in one hand and a cotton ball in the other.

She hangs up the phone. "What are you doing with that?"

He steps closer.

"No." She backs up against the register. "I don't..."

He douses the cotton ball with peroxide. The liquid spills down his hand and drips all over the floor.

"No." She crosses her arms.

He steps closer, squeezing the cotton ball and sets the peroxide bottle on the counter. His free hand brushes the bruise on her cheek.

Someone screams, out on the main street.

Anna nudges his hand away so she can see the front door. The street lights illuminate every inch of an empty street. Across the way, shadows litter the school campus. As a distraction, Anna asks James, "So the fire's out?"

"No." He doesn't cease, he doesn't pull away, or back down. He presses the cotton ball to her neck and wipes the cut left by the coke-head's blade.

It stings. Anna inhales through her teeth, thinking it will ease the discomfort. "James, what are you doing here?"

His fingers nudge her chin and he blows against the cut. A tingle rushes through Anna's veins. She inhales, deep. His thumb slides from her chin, across her lips. The register digs into her back, but she doesn't care.

Another person screams.

Something moves out of the corner of her eye—like someone sprinting past the front window.

She turns away from James, trying to get a better look at the street. The café's interior lights flood the place, reflecting off the glass—washing out the distant details of the campus.

"What"—he stands up, following her eyes —"was that?"

Anna's heart jerks. *The medical center.* Whatever it was—is happening—beginning—already started. Her heart races. *What am I gonna do? I gotta get home.*

Another scream comes. Someone darts past the window, going the same way as the last.

Anna and James look at each other.

Something hits the front window, like a water balloon exploding. A cheerleader in full uniform stands on the other side of the etched Eiffel Tower. Her palms press against the window, her eyes pierce the glass like she could tear into them—eat through them. Her lips are smeared red. *Is that ... blood?*

James grabs Anna's wrist, yanking her down behind the counter.

"What are you …?"

He shushes her, presses his back against the cabinets, leans his head around the edge of the counter, and peeks at the door, jerking his head back.

Shit. This is it. It's really happening. When am I going to wake up?

He looks at Anna's torn and patched scalp, patting a section of missing hair with the cotton ball.

Ouch. She knocks his arm away, but it returns, finding a new spot. *Ouch.* She inhales to ease the sting. He gets another spot. Anna gives up, letting him tend to her wounds as she concentrates on her racing heartbeat. Visions of horror movies and the idea of zombies, take hold of her thoughts.

James finishes. Anna attempts to stand to see what is going on outside, but James yanks her back down.

A light tap, like a bird pecking against glass, comes from the door.

James peeks around the counter and whips back. His eyes are wide. He spells something in what appears to be sign language.

I don't know that shit.

He slides closer, whispering in her ear, "I think she really wants a coffee."

"Maybe she came for the whipped cream," says Anna.

He smiles, leaning his head on her shoulder. The smell of his smoke-filled hair reminds her of a campfire, instead of the burning medical center. And something about that smell makes her realize the tapping at the door is not going away.

TIP TOES

ANNA MUST HAVE FALLEN ASLEEP. JAMES' BODY lurches from slumber, his head jerks away from her shoulder. Anna's ass is freezing from the floor and her neck is stiff from the weight of James' head. It is kind of funny how he startles. There is nothing like waking up and finding—

Toes sit at the edge of Anna's view—a pair of bare feet. Kelley stands over them, hunched, her hair stiff and messy. Long, clean-shaven legs lead up to a miniskirt. She dives down at Anna.

James swings his arm out, catching Kelley's chest, blocking a full-on attack. Kelley's fingers dig into Anna's arm, scratching a layer of skin off. Her teeth slide over the side of Anna's neck. James yanks Kelley back. Her bite eases.

Oh, my God she bit me. Anna's fingers frantically search for confirmation, touching the ring of saliva. *Ouch.* It hurts, but there isn't any blood. She inspects her fingers. *No blood.* Her heart sinks with relief.

James' yanks on Kelley, sending them both to the floor. He rolls on top of her, pinning both her arms. She snarls, trying to bite his face, then wrists. He looks at Anna. "What's wrong with her?"

I have no fucking idea. Anna stands up, looking for something—something to restrain her, stop her, bash her freakin' head in. She freezes.

Long, dark shadows stretch across the front window of the café outside. Pair after pair of eyes eat through the glass.

James lets out a loud grunt and then there is a *smack*. Kelley is knocked out, limp on the floor. James climbs to his knees, shaking out his wrists. "Well, she's going to be pissed with me late ... er."

The cheerleader's face is plastered against the front glass door. Her eyes widen to the point of falling out. She bangs her forehead against the glass with a soft thump.

Shit.

She does it again—thump.

James grabs Anna's hand.

Thump.

"You wouldn't happen to have an ax, would you?" Anna says, squeezing his hand.

"No. Where's the light switch?"

"Next to the door." Right next to the door. "And another by the backdoor."

The thumping morphs into a pound. It quickens, louder and louder. All the faces, pressed against the front window, stare at them. A second one—a kid in a football jersey—starts to bang his head against the glass. The guy beside him does it too. Then another. And another. The windowpane cracks.

A chunk of glass breaks from the door and shatters to the floor.

"Run," James says, letting go of Anna's hand.

The phone. Anna grabs a pen off the counter and jams it into the crack beside the register, grabbing Kelley's phone.

James runs into the back prep area.

Anna jumps over Kelley's pale, stiff body, knocking the stack of aprons to the floor, and kicks the whipped cream canister. The backdoor is wide open. *Shit.* Anna spins around. There is no one in sight. *James?* She hauls ass for the backdoor.

The wind gusts outside, brushing the treetops like they amount to nothing. The scent of fire fills the air.

Where is he? The parking lot is empty. *He left me?* The dumpsters are filled for tomorrow's pickup. There is no sign of her superhero. *He left me.*

The café window smashes to the floor inside.

Anna glances back over her shoulder. She has 30 seconds to make up her mind. That is it. *Where'm I gonna go?* Her pulse urges her to move forward—go somewhere—keep moving. *Home.* She will have to go down the alley and take the main stretch, before crossing the bridge to the trailer park. She digs her toes into the soles of her sneakers and pushes off the threshold, sprinting for the alleyway. *This is a stupid idea.* Intermittent gusts of wind tease the patches of her missing hair, making it hard to trust her decisions.

She makes it to the alley's edge. *I can't believe he left me.*

The alley is dark. Its shadows disappear at the end—another street's beginning. A man is hunched there, taking shelter from the wind. Newspapers tumble past. He doesn't move, doesn't give them a second glance. His hoodie is pulled tight and he coughs into his hand.

Anna steps into the alley, sprinting for its end, past him—waiting for him to grab her ankle, pull her down, and force himself through her veins.

Her shoes crush the cardboard that lay facedown beside him. She bursts past the edge of the wall—free—out into the open, a few feet west of the café.

Bodies file through the door and window, crushing the shards of glass beneath their feet. The last three in the mob, are a bunch of skinny dudes who look like they have escaped a *Magic the Gathering* tournament. One has a large gouge down his nose. A two-inch piece of glass protrudes from his friend's cheek. The chubbier of the three has a bloody handprint smeared across his forehead.

Anna runs for home. Each step pounds against the asphalt. She slips on a wet leaf here and there, requiring an adjustment to gain balance. *Look back. See how close their fingers are from grabbing your hair, ripping the shirt off your back, and sinking their teeth into your neck.*

No. Anna won't look back.

Jerry's glowing TATTOO sign catches her eye. She runs for it, rips the door open, pulls it closed, and prays no one has followed her.

The buzzing noise of an active tattoo gun fills the small waiting room.

Anna steps up to the front counter. "Jerry?"

His greasy hair hangs over a guy's arm. That is nothing new. He needs to wear glasses, but refuses to. The buzzing noise isn't coming from his hand though. It is coming from the tray behind him. The tattoo gun vibrates, bumping into little bowls of blue and black ink.

"Jerry?"

His head lifts. His bottom front teeth are missing. Blood drains between them, dripping down his chin. A chunk of the guy's arm is ... missing. Jerry chews on it. The guy in the chair is dead. *He's dead.*

Anna backs up, until her back hits the door. She startles, jumps, spins, and yanks the door open.

A guy who frequents the café enough to be familiar comes around the threshold. Anna bumps into his left shoulder, spinning him as she sprints out of there. His other arm ... is gone. Anna pushes herself as hard as she can for home—past the aqua door of the bar she knows so well. There is no way she is stopping again. *Screw that.* She moves off the sidewalk into the middle of the road. No way she is getting closer than six feet to anyone else.

Tires squeal a few blocks ahead, and a car pulls out. Its headlights blind Anna's view. She looks ridiculous running down the road, but doesn't give a crap how she looks. The car speeds closer.

She doesn't want to move out of the way—get near the sidewalk. Nor does she want to get in another strange car— neither James' van or Parker's little shit Beetle. *Assholes.*

The approaching vehicle doesn't slow. It charges full speed. Its silhouette morphs into a black Hummer. Of course it does.

No way. I'm not going to be dragged off, become a whisper of a child my mother once had. Anna veers to the right and the vehicle accommodates left, speeding past. Streetlights reflect off the orange biohazard logo of its door.

A sick feeling floods over Anna. She pushes her hands against bent knees, trying to breathe. Her lungs burn and the saliva in her mouth has thickened. She can't help but feel like this is all their fault. Whatever fucked up thing is happening, it has to do with them.

Another set of headlights comes up from behind Anna. *Not another one.* She glances back, blinded by the light. The headlights dart to the opposite lane as they pass, revealing a crappy sedan. The passenger window draws down. The streetlamp illuminates the glisten of a pistol.

Anna dives to the ground.

A shot fires, piercing the brick wall behind her. The driver yells out the window, "Die, zombie!"

Its taillights disappear into the distance and the street's eerie reverence floods in. Only the wind speaks, carrying the same air that legends once breathed.

FALLEN

ANNA CAN SEE THE BRIDGE TO THE TRAILER PARK IN the distance. The fog has settled against the ground, burying the town. Faint balls of light guide her down the road. She has reached the guardrail of the bridge that protects the creek below.

Headlights pop up over the hill, coming full speed. Lines of light shoot all around Anna. The driver swerves, hitting the guardrail and ricocheting back towards her.

Shit. She hops the guardrail behind her and falls. For a second she is flying. Her arms flop in the air above her and her feet sail through the fog. It's eight feet down. Her ass hits the water first, landing on a fist-size rock. Her sneakers sink into the mud and her hands smack the water. She retches with the pain.

The vehicle's left tire hangs off the bridge overhead, restrained by a bent guardrail. Dark smoke drifts up from the engine, disappearing completely into the fog.

Great. Anna shoves her fists into the mud, pushing off the rock. Her fingers slide through half-decayed leaves and worms. *Worms. I just fucking know it.* She schleps herself onto the steep bank.

Brakes screech above. Headlights trickle down, reaching for the rocks. A heavy engine growls, idling above. It is a bus. It decompresses, hissing, as the door cranks open.

A male voice follows, "Jesus."

Anna rests her bruised cheek against the mud. Someone will come down, drag her up, give her a hospital bed to sleep in. But there is no hospital, not anymore.

She doesn't hear the guy run over to the car above, but she hears him pull the driver's side door open.

He squeals, "Jesus. Um ... stay right there. I'll call it in. Just ..., just hang on."

He isn't going to save Anna. Why would he bother to look in the trenches, down there? She claws her way up the bank and climbs onto the asphalt.

The bus' headlights illuminate the car accident, washing out the silhouette's details. A guy falls out of the car. The bus driver sprints back to assist him, bracing his arm, helping him to stand.

The guy climbs to his feet, keeping his shoulders hunched. His right wrist is twisted. A bone protrudes out the side of his leg. He faces Anna, staring with a loose hanging jaw.

123

"Are you, okay," says the driver.

The guy shifts his attention from Anna to the bus driver.

The bus driver starts walking backward.

Run.

The wind rustles the treetops hiding behind the fog.

Run.

"How about ..." the bus driver holds out his hands, "you stay right there and I'll radio—"

The guy lunges, tackling the bus driver, biting into his forearm.

Anna runs for the trailer park.

The driver's screams ripple like a wave with each step. She has abandoned him. Each step drives the shame deeper through her heart.

Mom's trailer appears in the distance. Its detail crisps as Anna's sneakers pound against the asphalt. The wind blows against her cheeks, picking at the mud smeared across her skin.

She doesn't bother to check on the bickering couple or the old vegetable garden.

Megan is sitting on her trailer step, smoking a cigarette. Her eyes widen at Anna's presence and she shoots to a stand.

My hair, the scabs. Can she see my hair? Oh, who cares? Anna focuses on her trailer door. She can't wait to get in and lock it. Sleep for a few hours. Wake up to it all being a dream.

"Did those guys stop by your place?" Megan drops the cigarette, grinding it into the ground with her big toe.

Anna yanks her trailer's door open and slams it closed

behind her, collapsing against it.

Megan pounds on the outside. "I'm talking to you—"

Anna yanks open the door. "Megan, fuck you! You're a slut. You have a different guy over every week. I know your Dad fucked you when you were little, but shit. You don't have to be a complete and total whore." Anna takes a breath. "Don't be such a fucking bitch." She slams the door in Megan's face. *I shouldn't have said that.* It was supposed to feel good, to release the years of all the crap Megan said to her. But it didn't. Anna felt sick, disgusted with herself. *Is this how she feels? Disgusted? Worthless?* Anna leans against the door, waiting for Megan to come back, waiting for her nasty words to justify everything Anna said. But she doesn't. Anna leans a little harder against the door, sinking deeper with regret. *Shut up. She deserved it.*

"What are you doing?" says Jeremy from the kitchen.

"Um ..." Anna has nothing.

"What the hell happened?" His eyes ignore the mud dripping off her fingertips soiling the floor, and stares at her hair—the missing pieces.

"Are you okay?" He scoops her into his arms and squeezes her tight, pressing a hand against her muddy cheek, holding her head against his chest.

The tightness hurts but she endures it, resting in his arms.

"Anna?" he says.

She doesn't want to talk about it. She is too tired, so tired of her life.

He gives her a tight squeeze.

All of the night washes away. She is safe. She is home.

He eases her from his arms and heads for the coffee pot. "You want some?"

It is too late to drink coffee. Having a cup now would only fuel the thoughts racing around in Anna's head. *It isn't real.* The world isn't falling completely apart outside of the trailer walls. *I'm not crazy.*

Jeremy smiles at her.

If she has a cup of coffee, sleep will be unattainable. She will be up all night. *I'll be up all night.* "Yes."

Surprise tugs at the corners of Jeremy's eyes. He pulls a stack of coffee filters from the cabinet above. They stray from his grasp, raining down onto the counter. One drifts away from all the others, floating to the floor.

Anna scoops up the renegade and nudges Jeremy away from the coffee machine. "I'll do it."

He beams. To him, making coffee is Anna's job—her gift to the world—and one day she will open a café of her own. That is his dream for her, never considering that she has absolutely no interest in it at all. Anna never wanted to be a princess growing up. Why would she? She wanted to be Joan of Arc, until learning that the very people she protected burned her alive. Anna realized how impossible dreams are and settled for normal life.

Jeremy's hands shake as he slides the filters back into the cabinet.

"What's wrong?" asks Anna.

"Oh, nothing. Your mom bit me ..." Jeremy continues talking but the words fade to the background of Anna's thoughts.

Bit him? She scoops a spoonful of canned coffee and dumps it into the machine. *What?* She spoons another scoop into the filter. "She bit you?"

He takes the coffee pot to the kitchen sink, filling it with faucet water. "Do you know an Elizabeth Hutch—something?"

"Who?"

"Some girl with long blonde curls? Looks about your age." He crosses the kitchen and pours the water in the machine. "She's wanted by the cops. It's all over the news."

Anna shuts the top lid and hits the button. The name isn't familiar, but it is. Why do the blonde curls stand out in her mind? *The girl from the café? Those guys ... those Meadowlark guys?*

Jeremy pulls a half-spent joint from the junk drawer. He leans against the counter and digs into the pocket of his boxers, retrieving a plastic lighter. He lives in those things. Boxers with pockets cost a lot more. Last Christmas Anna found two pairs. She gave him the black plaid ones that are now grey, for his birthday. The other pair he will get for Christmas.

Anna doesn't see any sign that Mom bit him.

"You hear they shut down all the airports?" He lights the burnt end of the joint and sucks in deep. "They say there's some highly contagious flu going around, Z-twenty something. That's probably what's wrong with your mom." He offers out the joint.

Anna takes it. Smoking with Jeremy was weird at first. He's

a lot older than Anna and even though he is her dad—in every sense—it always feels like she is somehow cheating on Mom. Anna's mother is usually in the other room: watching TV, passed out, or talking to Aunt Kathy about something on social media.

Anna sits down on the floor, leaning her head back against the cabinet. A chill shoots through her, igniting the thought of the café, the fact that James is gone—that he left her—that she had been so stupid again. She sucks in the smoke, needing something to take her mind off it all. She passes the joint back to Jeremey, holding the smoke in her lungs. "Where'd she bite you?"

"On my fucking back." He sits down beside Anna, lifting the edge of his wife-beater.

Anna laughs. "I'm not even going to ask ..."

He smiles, lets go of his shirt, and takes the joint, enjoying it. Burnt embers fade into used charcoal, burning down the dried leaves inside.

The coffee machine hisses and liquid drains into its empty glass pot.

The deep feeling that indica cannabis plants bring, hits Anna's bloodstream and her anxiety eases. She loves the strains Jeremy chooses. They ease her head and calm her nerves. The sativa activates her paranoia and races her thoughts to mind popping speeds—something she needs no help with today. The pain of her scalp, cheek, and back ease. She stares at the trailer door. "Do you think we'll live through"—she looks at him—"whatever this is?"

The coffee above them on the counter trickles to a stop.

Anna stands up. She doesn't want him to think she's crazy. Die of the flu? *Shit.* Only sick people die of the flu. She pours the brown liquid into two mugs.

Jeremy climbs to his feet and spoons sugar into the owl one. The joint flops between his lips. "I think you're the strongest woman I know."

Anna wants to believe that.

The side of his lips turn up to a grin, and ash falls in a clump from the burning paper.

For a second he has fooled her, into believing she is more than the walls of this trailer, the faded ratty dreamcatcher in her room, the worn and dirty sneakers covering her feet. She stares at the mud caked to their laces and leans her head on his shoulder. "Thanks, Dad."

He lets it stay quiet for a moment, then sucks the joint down to the point of burning his fingers. He starts coughing like it is his first time smoking.

"Jeremy?" Anna lifts her head.

His face is turning red.

She darts to the sink, grabs a glass from the drying rack, and twists the faucet on.

His cough deepens.

Come on. The water takes its time filling the glass. At halfway, she yanks it out and rushes it over to him.

His hands shake against hers as he takes it, forcing it to his lips as another cough comes out.

The faucet behind her wastes water as she watches him empty the glass. The running water sounds nothing like a natural stream.

NYMPH

JEREMY DRAWS THE CUP DOWN FROM HIS LIPS AND leans his head back against the counter. His wife-beater is soaked. A cheap lighter falls from his pocket and slides across the floor.

Anna laughs. "You're like a damn virgin."

He looks down at the mess of his shirt and joins in the laughter. "Must be some good shit."

"I don't know," Anna says, helping him stand. "I think you scared me straight."

He wipes the sweat from his brow and grabs onto the counter to steady himself. Anna goes to shut off the running water. He takes a step and his weight shifts, swaying. She nods him toward the three-person table pushed up against the hallway wall. She returns to his sugar-filled owl mug. "I'll bring it over."

Jeremy takes the seat closest to the hallway and rests his head in his hands.

Anna has smoked long enough to just go with the flow. The best is smoking with new people, gauging their tolerance. But Jeremy has never coughed before. Anna is sure his lungs are fully caked with resin. The heat seeps through the mug she picks up, warming her palms. She delivers it to Jeremy and goes back for the milk.

"What's this?" he says, picking up the mug.

What?

"Water?"

Water? Anna grabs the milk carton and walks back over.

Jeremy lifts his head, tilting the cup. The color has washed out of his cheeks. His eyes are wide, staring at her. "That shit must've been good."

It can't be water. She slides the milk carton on the table, looking into the mug. The liquid is clear. *It can't be.* She takes it to the sink and dumps it. *It is—steaming water.* She runs over to the other coffee mug. *No....* There is a deep brown liquid in it, and still an inch of settled coffee remaining in the bottom of the brewed pot.

Jeremy stands up. The chair screeches as it digs into the floor. His steps are silent, but Anna can sense him coming up behind her, peering over her shoulder.

She cups her hands around the mug. The coffee inside swirls and the brown color begins to fade clear. She brings the cup closer. The coffee has turned to water. *Water.* She drops the mug.

It hits the floor. The handle cracks off and clear liquid splashes out.

Jeremy wipes his eyes, trying to see the image more clearly.

What the—? Anna cannot move.

His expression goes blank and he heads toward the hallway.

"Jeremy?" Anna says.

He stops beside the table.

"Dad?"

He grabs the milk carton and walks to her, holding it out, shoving it into her hands.

She doesn't want to take it, but she knows if she doesn't, he'll let it fall to the floor. Its weight sinks in her grip.

He takes it back and pours it out onto the floor. It is water.

Water. Anna can't breathe.

He looks at her like he has never met her before, stepping back, bumping into the table.

She looks down at her hands. They are shaking. *I don't understand. How ... how ...?* She stares past her fingertips at the puddle he has poured. "Jeremy?"

He sits down in the chair, sliding the half-spent milk carton beside him on the table.

"Dad ...?"

He shakes his head like he is trying to dislodge thoughts he doesn't want. "It'll be okay."

Anna doesn't believe that. She can tell he doesn't believe it either. She wants to scream at him in that moment, let out the fear beginning to suffocate her, but this isn't his fault.

He starts to cough, cupping his mouth with his hand and bracing his head with the other.

Anna slides into the seat across from him, pushing the milk carton toward him.

He takes it, still hacking, and presses it to his lips. Water spits from its edge, and his voice box squeaks, as he swallows. He slams the carton down onto the table coughing, trying to hold it in, but unable to contain it. Blood sprays like an exploded paintball.

Jesus. Anna shoots up from her seat and grabs the hand towel from the stove.

He coughs in the bend of his arm, reaching for the towel with the other, then shoves it in his mouth, easing the force of each cough until they taper to long, intermittent gasps of air.

A dark shadow appears behind him in the hall.

Anna's heart jumps. *Mom!* "Shit, you scared me." Anna's eyes shoot to the mess on the floor and back at her mother. Mom looks tired. The bags beneath her eyes sag more than usual. Her eyes don't bother to follow Anna's glance to the water mess.

Jeremy moans, keeping his face buried in the towel, breathing.

What am I going to tell her? Anna doesn't know what to tell her mother. She doesn't know what this is… *How is she going to look at me after all this?*

Jeremy leans his head back. Blood soaks through the hand towel. He coughs and droplets spray into the air.

A gun goes off—in Megan's house.

Mom leans forward and bites into the side of Jeremy's neck, digging her teeth deeper, tearing the artery out of his flesh.

Anna can't move. She wants to run, sprint for the door. But they are her family—her people. She can't take her eyes off the way her mother's stare locks at her from across the table. Blood drains down her lips. Jeremy cups the bite wound, but Mother tips his chair and he falls back. His head whacks the floor. She lunges past the table at Anna.

Mom?

She slips, grabbing Anna's ankle.

"Mom!"

Her fingernails dig into Anna's skin, yanking her an inch from falling off the edge of the chair. She should have kicked her mother off, but how could she? Mom's nails dig deeper and she jerks harder.

Mom. Anna can feel her mother's breath against her skin.

Someone is screaming. It is Anna. She can't feel her body. It is like watching someone else. She has become a bystander, too helpless to free the girl from the terror of her mother's assault.

The chair falls and Anna goes with it. Her back hits the floor, forcing her back into a reality that should never exist. She rolls, digging her fingers into the floor, trying to get to the front door. She stops screaming, but deep cries pour out.

Mom grabs hold of Anna's hair, yanking her head backward,

causing her to fall back on top of her mother. Mother's fingers tighten, pulling Anna's head back farther, closer to her teeth. Mom's breath is cold, chilling Anna's neck.

My artery. Her teeth are far too close. Anna screams, "Mom!"

The trailer door bursts open.

Megan storms in with a long-barrel handgun, presses it against Mom's temple, and pulls the trigger.

DRAGONFLY

THE TIPS OF MOM'S FINGERS FALL LOOSE FROM ANNA'S
skin. Her body falls limp beneath Anna's back.

No. Anna rolls off, waiting to be eaten and torn apart by the
woman who created her. She rolls, unable to process what
Megan did. She rolls not to feel the cold corpse of her mother
beneath her. Jeremy's blood drains out between Mom's teeth.
No. Anna turns away. She can't see her mother like that. She
shoots to her feet, closing in on Megan, screaming, "What did
you do?"

Megan lets the gun droop in her hand as she sinks to the floor. Confidence melts down her cheeks. She shakes the moment of self doubt from her head and raises the weapon, pointing it at Anna.

Anna stops. She knows Megan can kill her, finish-off all the damage her words have already done. Anna takes a long breath and steps closer. She wants Megan to do it. She has feared death for far too long, wasted so much time drowning in it. She says, "Do it."

Megan's stance softens.

Anna steps closer, forcing Megan to push on the gun to keep her distance back. She longs to be with Mom and Jeremy—Dad. She steps, forcing the barrel to push into her cheek, harder, saying, "Do it."

Megan lowers her eyes, clears her throat, and looks at Anna's patchwork hair. "What the fuck happened to you?"

Out of everything—everything she has to point out Anna's fucking hair. She has just killed Anna's mother.

Anna longs to glance back, to make sure her mother is dead, but she can't. She can't look back again to pay any kind of respect. Nausea pushes up from the bottom of her stomach and she fights to keep it down. Tears leak from her eyes. She doesn't want to feel the pieces of her soul slide down her face. She wipes them so harshly, fingernail marks slice down her cheek.

Megan withdraws the gun from Anna's face and heads for the trailer door. She walks away, leaving Anna there, leaving them all there.

"Where the fuck do you think you're going?" Anna runs up behind Megan, ramming her shoulder into Megan's back.

Megan goes flying—skidding across the living room rug. The gun disappears beneath the couch.

Anna pounces on Megan, wraps her fingers around her throat, and squeezes. Megan chokes. Blood rushes to her face. It would be as easy as squeezing a water balloon—to pop Megan's head off. Anna tightens her grip around Megan's throat. The blood vessels in Megan's eyes bulge. *What am I doing?* Anna lets go.

Megan chokes in gasps, rolls to her stomach, and barfs all over the rug.

Anna dives beside her, reaching beneath the couch, frantically feeling for the gun. It isn't there. She can't find it. She swings her arm in the opposite direction, jamming her shoulder up against the couch, stretching her fingers a little farther.

Megan climbs to all fours.

Anna reaches deeper, harder, further beneath the couch. Her fingertips bump metal. *There it is.*

Megan lets out a grunt behind Anna.

Anna rolls to see what she is doing.

Megan's fist smashes down on Anna's stomach.

Anna's lungs empty with one grunt. Her stomach tightens, forcing her to sit up, jerking her shoulder out of socket. Screams explode from her lips.

The open front door bangs against the kitchen wall. Cold air floods in.

Megan freezes.

Anna's body sinks back to the floor. Her fucking shoulder hurts so bad. Tears roll out of her eyes, blurring the figure now standing in the doorway. She squints, moistening her eyes to see the image of a scrawny kid standing in the threshold. It is the young teenager who lives at the cul-de-sac's edge. He spends the weekend sitting on the front steps of his trailer playing on his phone. His ball-cap is always turned backward. When the noon sun pivots overhead, he'll squint for hours instead of flipping his cap the right way. It still sits backward on his head, but now has deep sweat stains. Drool drips from his off-centered lip-ring. One eye hangs loose from its socket. The other eye darts past Megan—directly at Anna who is still pinned beneath the couch. Anna is no match for some hormone-filled teenage zombie. She reaches deeper beneath the couch. His moan morphs into a growl.

"Shit!" Megan whispers, unmoving.

Anna turns her attention back to the couch, pressing up against, forcing another inch of reach beneath it.

Behind her, one of them falls to the floor with a thump.

Shit. Where is it? Anna searches the spot she thinks it should be. It's not there. She pulls her arm out, smashes her cheek to the floor and looks beneath the couch. It is dark, but faint Halloween lights reflect off the gun's metal. Anna shoves her arm back under the couch, searching that same spot. *Where is it?* She wants to turn around—to see how close the kid has come, and judge the minutes until he kills her. She stretches the tips of her fingers a little farther.

Nothing.

No. For a moment, she gives up, lays still, and lets the monster of defeat devour her—take her away from this hellhole. Her hand drops completely, giving up—only for a second—and her knuckles rest on the pistol. Her heart jumps. She hooks a finger around its trigger guard, yanks the gun out from beneath the couch, rolls, aims it at the closest figure, and pulls the trigger.

One of them falls.

She aims at the other. Her finger loosens on the trigger enough to load the next bullet.

Megan stands over the dead boy, too in shock to move.

Anna could do it, just tighten her finger on the trigger.

Megan's eyes make their way to Anna's.

The gun Megan killed Anna's mother with is probably Hector's. Megan's eyes confirm to Anna that the shot from earlier had been hers. She had done it. She killed one of her own. Megan lets out a breath and holds out her hands, palms open, surrendering. They are covered in dry blood.

No. I won't have pity on her. She deserves everything that comes her way. She's made my life hell for ... for forever. Anna has spent so many nights crying into her pillow because of Megan.

"Anna," Megan pleads.

Childhood memories race through Anna's mind. The adrenaline pulsing through her veins calms, letting the pain of her heartbreak flood back in. Her body aches.

Blood seeps from the boy's torso, pooling beneath him.

Anna doesn't have to look down. She doesn't want to look down. So she looks down the barrel of the gun, at Megan. The gun shakes in her hands, weaving back and forth across Megan's frame.

I killed him. Anna lowers the gun and glances down at the thick liquid oozing out of the kid's wound. *No.* Anna forces her eyes away—to Megan and past her—at the floor beside the counter, at Mom's lifeless fingertips. Anna zones out, somehow making it outside. Mist splashes her cheeks as she strides down the steps.

Megan could jump out of the trailer and pound against Anna's back, hit her, wound her, kill her, but Anna doesn't care. Megan comes full force out the door and down the steps.

Anna freezes, letting it happen.

Megan stops right behind Anna. Her breath blows against the back of her neck as her mouth opens, readying the words that will spill out.

Anna closes her eyes. She doesn't want to deal with anything, especially after what just happened. Anna will let Megan kill her. It is what she deserves. Anna takes a step. Water molecules pop against her cheek in the mist. Anna can feel Megan standing in place, frozen behind her. She takes another step, rhythmically heading for the bus stop.

"Wait," Megan says in reverent voice—the same tone Anna imagines her words would sound like if she could speak. "Why don't we take Hector's car?"

We? Anna faces her, looking at the vehicle in their driveway. It is some kind of muscle car convertible stuffed beneath a tarp. Ten months out of the year it is stored, top down with a tarp thrown over it. Autumn's late arrival last week gave Hector one more month of use over prior years.

Megan doesn't look back as she makes her way to the car, pulling the tarp off. A puddle of rainwater above the driver's seat dumps into the interior. She tugs the tarp harder, dragging it across the yard.

November's new wind pushes in, taking away the possibility of dreams, making it so real.

A dark-grey owl sits perched on the storage shed at the foot of the driveway. A bright light flashes over its yellow, glowing eyes.

Headlights cut through the fog behind them. James' VW van shoots straight toward them.

Anna's heart jerks. *Son of a—*

The owl screeches.

Her heart jerks again and her body jumps.

The van skids to a halt on Megan's lawn. Anna wants him to be bloody and half-dead, so she has a good reason to shoot him.

He jumps out of the vehicle complete with firefighter gear.

"Damn," says Megan, heading toward him. Leave her to be the one to think about sex in an apocalypse. Her shoulder brushes Anna's as she passes. She begins to introduce herself, holding out a hand.

James pays no attention, swirling around her, headed for Anna.

The weight of the gun hangs in her hand, but she can't lift it. He grabs her arms. Her heart pounds at his touch.

He shakes her. "Where did you go?"

"You left me!" Anna karate-chops his hands off with one swoop and draws the gun to his face. It vibrates with anxiety. "I almost died."

Megan comes up beside him. "Twice. You almost died twice."

He grabs Anna's wrists, pulls her up against his chest, and presses her head against him.

Anna sinks into his embrace for only a second and almost cries. *No.* She pushes him back. "You don't get to comfort me. You left me!"

"Guys…" Megan says.

"I trusted you," Anna says. "It was so stupid. And you left me, just like…" *The guy at the park.* Her heart beats, pounds the blood through her veins, reminding her of the bruise on her cheek and the cut down her back. "I was meeting a guy at the park, okay?" *Alright? There, you happy I said it? I told you everything.* "I was going to fuck some guy in the park. An older guy ... someone with money to get me out of this dump."

"Guys ..." Megan says.

"But some crackhead was there. He ..." *I can't...* The words choke in her throat. *Could this be who I am?* "The guy showed up. He left me." Her stomach cramps. *Oh God, I said it.* "He left me to be raped by some crackhead." *There. Happy now? Satisfied that I'm the piece of shit trailer park trash you thought I was?* She looks him square in the eye. "You left me!"

His hands drop away, no longer making any attempt to touch her.

"Anna!" Megan yells.

Anna glances at her.

She nods, past James, at the Quinns' trailer.

Mr. Quinn stands in the streetlight of his front yard, frozen, holding the end of a water hose that isn't on. He walks toward them, dragging it.

Megan's voice is soft, "Get in the car."

The living room blinds of Ms. Murphy's trailer part. Anna can't see the old woman, but she knows she is in there, looking out. She can't leave Ms. Murphy in there to die all alone. Anna sprints for her trailer.

Mr. Quinn's walk morphs into a hunt.

Anna can take a shot, but she isn't stupid. She doesn't

actually know how to shoot a gun. Who the hell knows what will happen if she tries? She calculates the amount of hose left, the approximate circumference of the safe zone, and veers right —crossing into its safety.

But Mr. Quinn lets go of the hose. There is no recoil. He careens into Anna, knocking her in the opposite direction.

Her elbow hits the asphalt. It tears at her skin as she skids. Her shoulder and temple whack the pavement, scraping against it like sandpaper. A ringing noise pierces her eardrums. She lay there, unable, unwilling to move. She can't tell which anymore. She should've shot the bastard.

James slides his arms beneath hers, pulling her to her feet.

Mr. Quinn has regained his stance, three feet in front of them.

Anna aims the gun and pulls the trigger. It kicks back and she re-aims at his head, waiting for the fucker to move.

Mrs. Quinn comes out of nowhere—from the thick fog—and lands on Megan, biting into her leg. Megan screams. Mrs. Quinn spits a piece of flesh out and takes another bite.

James runs over, punching Mrs. Quinn in the back of the head. A gust of wind blows by, cutting the fog and breaking his trance. He sinks to the rain-soaked ground, leaning back on his hands to catch his breath.

Megan's screams subside to loud cries and alternating curses.

Ms. Murphy's trailer door flings open. She descends the steps slowly, carrying a shotgun. Anna can't believe her eyes. Even Megan stops whining. Ms. Murphy pulls a handkerchief from the deep pockets of her flower-print nightgown and throws it at Megan. She looks at Anna and nods at James, "Give him the gun."

No. Anna isn't going to hand over the only thing that can keep her alive. The thing that ... killed Mom.

Ms. Murphy rests a hand on Anna's shoulder. "Go ahead."

Anna's head sinks and she does as instructed. She doesn't really want the gun anyway. She hands it over James.

His fingers slide through the mud as he crawls to a stand, taking it from her. He glances at Megan. His words soften, "I'll get the van."

Anna watches him walk back toward the van parked outside of Megan's trailer. The faded dreamcatcher in Anna's bedroom window sways as the heater vent kicks on, urging her not to leave, warning her that she will never return.

James gets in the van and stops to pick the women up—Anna's one-way ticket out of there.

Ms. Murphy walks back toward her garden boxes.

"You're not leaving me, are you?" says Megan. Her fingers shake as she knots the handkerchief around her leg. "You can't leave me."

Ms. Murphy kneels down beside the first garden bed, leans the shotgun against it, and pulls something from the soil.

"Anna?" says Megan.

Anna doesn't want to look at her, let Megan's eyes sucker her into being the pathetic, sympathetic, weak person Anna always is. She looks back at their trailers, their adjacent driveways.

Once upon a time, chalk flowers spanned both sides, shared

equally in patterns. Until Megan's dad showed up, moved in, and parked his car in the driveway.

Anna looks at the girl she had spent countless hours dreaming about the future with. She glances back at the trailer—the dreamcatcher that has saved her from nightmares. All at once Anna scoops Megan up off the ground and drags her ass toward the van.

James steps in front of them, blocking the door. "I don't think —"

"I can't leave her." Anna knows what he is going to say: that he doesn't think they should take her with them. She had made Anna's teenage years hell. The past five years have been shit, but... Anna looks down at Megan, her bloody handkerchief, and looks James square in the eyes. "It will kill me if I do."

He points the gun at Megan's head and pulls the trigger.

He...

Megan's body falls limp in Anna's arms. Anna lets go, lets Megan's corpse slip from her hands. Blood drains from her dead body, bleeding into the soil beneath Anna's feet.

He ... Anna looks at James. *He left me. He left me after the café.* He shot her. Anna's feet won't move. She doesn't want to leave the cul-de-sac she's grown up on, get in a van with him. She backs away.

"What are you doing?" He climbs into the driver's seat. "Get in."

THE OLD WOMAN

ANNA GETS INTO THE VAN. THE TRAILER PARK MELTS behind them.

Ms. Murphy settles into the front passenger seat.

Anna scoots to the edge of the backseat, wanting to ask: where they are going, why the hell aren't they heading back into town. Instead, she sits back, sinking into the seat.

Small fires light up the distance ahead. Looters swarm the streets. A man runs out in front of the van. James slams on the brakes. Anna's ass slides off the seat and her head whacks the back of the driver's seat.

A chubby businessman pounds against the side door window. "Let me in!"

The engine revs. The van shoots forward and hits something, bouncing over it, crushing it into the road.

Oh, my God. Was that a…? Anna spins around, watching a man convulse in the road behind them. *It was a person.* "You ran him over!"

James' eyes remain fixed on the road, avoiding the rearview mirror.

Something large appears in the distance. The dark silhouette morphs into the lines of a spaceship as we get closer. A sign on the right declares it: *private property of McAllister Industries.* The spacecraft is suspended in air by a tower. It is a contemporary two-story building, framed with windows.

James pulls up to the front of the building, parking like a valet beneath a grand awning fit for a hotel. He glances in the mirror at Anna, hops out, and heads for a set of glass doors.

Ms. Murphy and Anna slide out of the van simultaneously. The old lady offers the shotgun to Anna.

No way is she taking that thing. It is three times the size of the handgun, three times more likely she will end up shooting herself accidentally.

"Relax," Ms. Murphy says. "It's not loaded."

Anna takes it. *Wait … Why the hell would she even bother offering the shotgun if it's not even loaded?*

Ms. Murphy winks, digging into her pocket. "Butterscotch?"

If Anna ate anything, she'd vomit. *How is it Ms. Murphy is so calm?* Anna glances back at the burning skyline in the distance. *This isn't happening.*

Ms. Murphy uncurls her wrinkled fingers, revealing the contents of her hand. A single candy rests among shotgun shells.

Anna takes it.

The wrapper sinks—disappears—into a small puddle of water.

Shit.

Ms. Murphy's eyes widen and race to meet Anna's. Her mouth gapes open.

The candy has turned to water. It has happened. There is no way to explain it or convince Ms. Murphy it had not happened. Anna's stomach twists.

"Dragonfly," says Ms. Murphy.

Instinctively Anna reaches for the cotton covering the tattoo on her breast. *How does she...know?*

A scream breaks from the distance.

Anna searches the fog, waiting for another, waiting to pinpoint its location, waiting for some fucker to materialize and kill them both.

It is silent.

Ms. Murphy starts for the building.

Wait. Anna hurries to join her. "How did you...? What does that mean? What is 'dragonfly'?"

James is already at the door, his hand is pressed against a keypad that sits right of the door.

It flashes red.

Anna glances back at the fog. It thickens, threatening to suffocate them.

"It's me," he says, waving his hands at a camera above the door. "For Christ's sake."

Ms. Murphy walks up beside him.

Fuck that. Anna stays put. The awning hides the spaceship from view. She doesn't know what could be inside, but it isn't an inviting building or place.

Ms. Murphy places a hand on James' shoulder and offers him something.

He takes it. His eyes stick to hers. He opens his mouth to say something, but nothing comes out.

The camera moves, tilting down to get a better look at the object.

A woman bursts through the visibility line of the fog to Anna's left. Her eyes grow wild at the sight of Anna. She starts screaming for help.

A zombie-woman pops out of the fog from behind her, tackles her to the ground, rips her voice box out, and claws her to pieces. The screams cease.

Shit.

The zombie lifts her head, digs her nails deeper into the dead woman's flesh, and comes at Anna like a hyena. Anna pivots, to run the other way, but is too slow. The zombie grabs Anna's shoulder, pulling her back. Anna falls to the ground, knocking the woman away. All the air heaves out of Anna's lungs on impact. The worthless shotgun slips from her hand. The woman's cracked, broken fingernails dig into Anna's thigh, yanking the flesh toward her bloody mouth.

The shotgun fires.

The fingernails digging into Anna's flesh ease and loosen, falling away. The zombie is dead.

Anna's ears ring from the blast.

Ms. Murphy says something inaudible and reaches down to help Anna up.

"I thought you said it wasn't loaded," Anna yells, taking Ms. Murphy's hand.

She hoists Anna up. A smile spreads across her lips. "In a mad world, it's good to be able to get a little crazy sometimes."

The front doors burst open. Two female Meadowlark Agents step out. It is the agents from the trailer park.

Crap. Anna digs her heels into the ground. *Nope. I'm not going in there.*

Agent Glenn's ponytail sways as she grabs the shotgun from Ms. Murphy.

Agent Sam crosses her arms and focuses on James. "I see you've finally come to your senses."

What's that supposed to mean? Anna doesn't want to stay to find out. She turns, digging her heels into the ground, and forces all her energy into running away.

Ms. Murphy grabs Anna's arm, catching her on the first step, yanking her back.

No. Anna's feet slide out from underneath her. She regains balance.

Agent Sam tackles her to the ground, twisting her thin wrists behind her back, ratcheting handcuffs around them. The agent forces Anna to stand and pushes her forward, toward the building's entrance.

James and Ms. Murphy have already disappeared inside, cooperating or dead.

Agent Glenn opens the door.

Anna stops.

Agent Sam shoves her in.

James stands in the middle of a two-story foyer. On the floor beneath him, 'AI' is carved.

McAllister Industries.

A hallway straight ahead separates two offices on each side. A secretary desk guards the hallway entrance. The office doors and walls that hug the lobby are glass—the only glass in the building. The ceiling stretches past a second-story conference room, creating a skyline of windows. Rain pounds against them.

James keeps his gaze on the light upstairs—the balcony above the secretary desk.

A woman slides out from behind the desk to greet James. Her teeth are as white as the bleached suit she wears. Her hair is freshly dyed platinum blonde, tainting her natural complexion. She approaches him. "Ah"—she grabs his face, pulls him close, and kisses his cheek—"I see we have to have an apocalypse to get a visit."

"I don't have time for this," he says. "Where's Mr. Pierson?"

She licks her thumb, smearing the grime off James' cheek. "Your father's in a meeting."

"What do you mean?" James' voice raises. "The world's falling apart out there—"

"Well!" a man yells from the open balcony above, leaning his bloated business suit against the railing. "Have you come to accept my offer?"

"I don't know if you've noticed, but the world is going to shit out there," says James. "Or have you been too busy to notice?"

Mr. Pierson's beady eyes shoot toward Anna. A smirk pulls at the corners of his mouth. He disappears from the guardrail and heads down the upstairs hallway.

Ms. Murphy rests on a leather couch off to the right.

An elevator pings behind the secretary's desk.

Mr. Pierson waddles out toward them, nodding as he passes the secretary. She stands down, returning to the desk, typing away at the computer. He holds out his empty palm to James.

James hands over the thing Ms. Murphy gave him. It is a single, fluid piece of metal, bent into an intricate dragonfly.

Mr. Pierson's eyes search Ms. Murphy and move on to Anna, saying to James, "Where did you get this?"

James glances back at the old woman.

Mr. Pierson steps up to him. "You have three hours."

Three hours? Anna looks at James for a sign of explanation, but he makes no effort to make eye contact. She asks, "Three hours for what?"

A sharp twinkle forms in Mr. Pierson's eyes.

James storms into the left office and flicks on the light. An enormous dragonfly covers its back wall. It looks identical to the one Pierson took, only way, way bigger. James heads straight for a large desk, flinging open its drawers.

Mr. Pierson heads back to the secretary. They carry on in conversation as Anna heads into the office after James. She wants to know what the hell he is doing, why he has brought them here, and what the fuck is happening in three hours, but a picture across the room sucks all her attention.

The photograph has an orange tint to it, like it had been taken a decade ago. It captures two young girls, maybe eight and ten years old, sitting beside a lake. They look alike, except the younger one has blue eyes and blonde hair, instead of brown. Kinky curls stick out from a loose ponytail, tied with a pink ribbon. Her mouth is half full with teeth and a saggy turtle sits in her hands. She looks familiar. Anna gets closer, stepping on some papers James knocked to the floor. Anna searches the room for any other pictures, but there are none. She grabs the picture frame, pulling it closer. *I know her. But from where?*

James huffs, defeated that he cannot find whatever it is he is looking for. He takes a step back to open another drawer. Glass cracks beneath the paper.

Anna nudges him off, shuffling the papers with the tip of her sneaker until a broken picture frame is revealed. This one is smaller. Anna carefully pulls it out.

Pictured are the same girls—now young women. The little blonde with the curls—is the girl from the café. It is Dominic's girl. The girl Meadowlark is looking for.

Anna drops the picture frame.

James looks back at her and down at the picture.

Chills rush up her spine as she stares at him. *Who are you?*

He reaches for the picture.

"What's in three hours?" she asks.

"The spaceship leaves," says Mr. Pierson, leaning in the doorway.

CAPTURE

MR. PIERSON WALKS AWAY. THE TAP OF HIS SHOES echoes in the lobby, stopping near the secretary desk.

Her typing ceases. She acts as if the world isn't falling apart —business as usual.

James takes the picture, slides it on the desk, grabs Anna's hand, and pulls her toward the chair. "You might want to sit down."

She doesn't resist. It is about damn time for answers.

He begins to pace, twisting his dreads. "We—my Dad's company—was hired to build Oasis, a place for humanity to survive."

"Survive what?"

He ceases pacing and lets go of his dreadlock, biting his nails. "The apocalypse."

It's not the... Anna waits for him to laugh, to show a sign that he is making it all up. *It can't really be...*

"The zombie apocalypse," he says.

She wants to laugh, call his bullshit out. But instead, it sinks in. She slouches deeper into the chair, looking at the picture. "What about her?"

He leans on the desk.

"Why do they want her?"

"That doesn't matter." He straightens up and clears his throat. "They're not going to be able to find her fast enough to fix this mess."

Mr. Pierson has returned to the doorway. "Spilling all our family secrets yet?"

James looks away, avoiding his father's gaze, or mine. His eyes dart to the dragonfly on the wall, motioning toward it. "You want to tell her how some fucking dragonfly..." He glances at her. "How some fucking dragonfly will save you in space?"

Mr. Pierson straightens up and steps into the office. A smirk chokes his already fat, red cheeks. "Water."

Water? Anna's heart jumps at the word. Blood rushes to her cheeks, igniting them in blush. The tips of her ears burn red.

"Cheryl!" Mr. Pierson leans his head back into the lobby, yelling at the secretary. "Bring me the donuts from the break room."

159

Her high-heels click through the empty building, fading away from them.

Mr. Pierson approaches Anna.

James stiffens, but doesn't move.

Pierson stops a foot from James.

The noise of Cheryl's heels precedes her entrance. She enters with the box of donuts, squeezes past Mr. Pierson, and tosses it onto the desk. Mr. Pierson holds out his chubby little fingers and she hands over a large knife—a hunting knife.

"Dad," says James. "What are you doing?"

Mr. Pierson leers, staring at Anna over James' shoulder. "Sometimes you wait your whole life for something. And one day—plop—it falls right into your lap."

Anna squirms. She doesn't know where the fuck this is going, but it isn't good.

"Would you like a donut?" Pierson says, stepping to the side of James and flipping the top of the box open for Anna.

"No, thank you," she says.

"What are you, some health freak like my son? Too good to eat shit?" He looks at James. "Too good to be anything like your Dad?"

"Dad ..." James says.

Pierson scoops out a donut with one hand and points the knife at Anna. "Too good to be like everyone else?"

Cheryl squeezes past him for the door.

Ms. Murphy steps in, blocking the secretary's way out. "So much anger comes from your generation."

"See ...?" Pierson says, glancing at James.

Ms. Murphy directs her words to Pierson. "You had your chance to change the world."

He lowers his hands slightly, surprised the words are for him.

"Now look at it." She walks over.

He redirects the knife to her.

She reaches for the donut in his hand and slides her fingers into its center. The frosting melts into water and the donut explodes like a water balloon, soaking Mr. Pierson's sleeve.

Oh my God. She ... she's a .... Anna blinks several times, trying to clear the image—see the donut again. *She's like me....*

James' mouth falls open, but his eyes don't twinkle with surprise.

A dark shadow fills Mr. Pierson's stare. He punches Ms. Murphy in the side of the head.

She falls to the floor.

He screams at Cheryl, "Roll her over! I want to see it for myself."

Cheryl's hands shake as she kneels beside the worn old woman, rolling her.

Oh my God. She's dead. Anna has to see for herself, she has to check. She pushes past James to get to Ms. Murphy.

Mr. Pierson swings, knocking Anna away.

"Dad!" yells James.

"You learn your place," yells Pierson. His face flashes red. He points a fat finger at his son. "Now!"

James tightens his lips and balls his fists.

Mr. Pierson wipes the sweat from his forehead, bends down on one knee, and cuts the front of Ms. Murphy's nightgown, rippling it open.

Her skin is pale with dark age-spots. Nipples hang at the bottom of wrinkled pancakes. On her left breast is a dragonfly tattoo.

Defy

"LOAD HER UP," SAYS PIERSON.

Cheryl grabs the old woman's wrist and drags her body toward the door.

No. I need to ask her things…. Anna makes for her.

James swings his arm out, restraining her.

She pushes her weight against him. "No. I need to know. I need to know what—"

Mr. Pierson's head whips around. He rolls his shoulders back and holds the knife out in front of him. "Strip."

What?

James' arm weakens, as surprised at the comment as her. He steps in front of her. "She's not doing anything."

Pierson moves fast and fluid. He takes one swing at James and knocks him out. Before Anna can escape, Pierson's fat little fingers twist into the fabric of her shirt, jerking her closer. "You do it"—saliva spits all over her face—"or I'll do it."

Asshole. Anna glances down at James.

He moans, busy peeling himself off the floor, soothing the bruise forming along his jaw.

Mr. Pierson presses the knife against Anna's throat.

Fuck this shit. She swings her hand back, balls her fingers, and punches the fucker in his fat face.

He barely moves. His head turns to one side, but that is it. His beady eyes swell with fury. "You bitch!"

Shit.

He hits back like a jackhammer.

Anna goes flying backward, crashing onto the desk, crushing the donut box. The broken picture-frame crunches beneath her spine and cuts into her skin as she rolls off.

James stands, broadening his shoulders, barricading Anna from the monster he served them to. His fingers roll into fists. "We are done."

Pierson grabs a handful of James' dreadlocks and yanks him closer. "You think it would be that easy? You think it would ever be that easy?"

James moans. Anna knows that feeling—the feeling that your entire scalp is going to be torn off and thrown into a bloody heap on the floor.

Pierson yanks harder, drawing James closer, digging his free hand into his own pocket, pulling something out. In one sweep, he shoves it down against James' leg.

James convulses and his body instantly goes limp.

Pierson holds a Taser, guarding himself from Anna. "Now!" His face boils red and spit spews between their distance. "Strip."

Anna leans against the desk, letting a piece of glass slice through her shirt. "No."

The red of his face deepens.

She can't hide the smirk breaking free—the reward of crawling beneath his skin, tearing a hole through his inflated ego.

He hits her with the Taser.

Everything goes black.

DARKNESS

ANNA'S HEAD THROBS. SHE OPENS HER EYES, BUT everything is black—pitch black. *Shit.* Her heart races, pounding against her ribcage to get out. Each breath is tight. *The tattoo.* She feels for her shirt. It is still intact, but she feels violated, like the fat motherfucker had rubbed his fingers all over her tattooed breast.

"Anna?" Ms. Murphy's voice cuts through the abyss, across from her.

The floor jerks and moves. They are in some kind of vehicle.

"Ms. Murphy?"

Warm fingers touch Anna's, cupping them.

Relief fills her. The darkness dulls a little, even if only in her mind.

"The dragonfly…" The words catch in Ms. Murphy's throat. "You can't leave."

What? "What do you mean I can't leave? Leave what?"

"Earth," she says.

"Leave Earth?" *What? Why would I…?* "How the hell would I do that?"

"Did anything seem out of place?" she says. "You have a gift —an extremely powerful gift. To turn things into water—the most precious and pure thing on this planet—in this universe. It is a gift. It is the greatest gift. Do not hide from it."

The building's spaceship-silhouette becomes clear in Anna's thoughts. She opens her mouth to ask Ms. Murphy how it is possible, why Anna can't control it. There is so much she needs answers to.

The vehicle slows.

There isn't enough time to ask more than one question. Anna searches for the old woman's eyes in the dark, but the lightless spectrum won't cooperate. "Why me?"

"Because you made the choice," she says.

"What do you mean I made a choice? I never asked for this. I never accepted some…" The Native in the café replaces the spaceship in her mind. The dark draws a crisp image of the turquoise beads and eagle feather wrapped in his bright white hair.

She squeezes Anna's hand.

"I didn't accept anything." Anna pulls away. *She's wrong.* Anna hadn't accepted this. *It was a drawing, just a tattoo.* Without Ms. Murphy's touch, the space goes cold all around her. She stares into nothingness.

The vehicle rolls over something—something big enough to bounce Anna into the air. Her body comes down and her hand flys out, hitting the old woman's.

Ms. Murphy grabs Anna's wrist—hard. "What was written beside the dragonfly?"

"How…?" *How the hell did she know?* Anna doesn't mean for the question to escape, to give any clue that she is right in the assumption.

The hum of the tires beneath them—moving, speeding toward a destination both have not chosen—jolts Anna's heart. Their time together is growing short.

"Bloodwort," says Anna.

Ms. Murphy doesn't say anything.

The tires screech. The vehicle cuts to the right. The women slide in the back, landing up against the wall, and into each other. Ms. Murphy wraps her arms around Anna, drawing the girl's face against her chest.

Anna savors the moment, taking the last burst of love Ms. Murphy has left to give. She holds onto her, resting her head against the old woman's chest. It is a comfort—an embrace Anna hasn't felt since childhood. It is something she hasn't given in years. "What's going to happen to us?"

"Anything," says Ms. Murphy.

That isn't an answer. Not something Anna wants to hear. She wants Ms. Murphy to know, to have answers—an inkling of what it is she fears, an idea of what is coming.

The vehicle that captured them slams to a halt. They tumble to the back doors. The driver's side door creaks open and shut. Then the passenger's. The lock of the back squeaks and the doors fling open, spraying them with bright, blinding light.

The two female agents stand silhouetted by floodlights.

Agent Sam's broad shoulders block Ms. Murphy from exiting. Her nose-ring twinkles as she looks at her partner, then grabs Ms. Murphy's ankle, yanking her out of the back.

Butterscotch candies and shotgun shells spill to the ground.

Agent Glenn tightens her ponytail and blocks the blinding light before Anna, allowing her eyes to adjust.

Behind the agents stands an enormous metal tower, reaching into the sky. A platform and a spaceship—five times the size of the last—take up every inch of view.

The spaceship is wider than those Anna has seen in history text books. *McAllister Industries, AI*, takes up the entire length of its side.

Ms. Murphy grunts as Agent Sam tries to pull her off the ground. Her eyes find Anna's. Fear has taken full control of her.

Her words, *"Don't leave Earth,"* spread through Anna's thoughts. It is the fear of leaving Earth that fills the old woman.

Ms. Murphy's fingers dig into the soil. She screams at Anna, "You have to stay!"

Anna looks at the spaceship. She has waited her entire life to get out of the trailer park. Now, all she wants is to do is go home, smoke a joint with Jeremy, and pass out. In the morning Mom will be there, spewing alcohol breath into her face. Leaving Earth means breaking the barrier—the line of life into the abyss of space. *There is no air in space.* Anna's heart pounds, choking her lungs.

Agent Sam yanks Ms. Murphy to her feet.

Ms. Murphy wiggles loose from her grip and leans toward Anna. "Follow the signs."

Signs? What signs? All Anna sees is a big ass spaceship, the kind you imagine in some sci-fi shit. Anna never understood how sci-fi characters chance it—leave Earth for the possibility of instant death? There are so many things that can go wrong, so many ways space can suck your breath away.

Agent Sam jerks Ms. Murphy away. The old woman winks at Anna, then punches the agent in the side of the face. Agent Sam loses balance and falls. Agent Glenn grabs hold of Ms. Murphy's fist and fumbles to get a pair of handcuffs on her. Ms. Murphy swings her head forward, head-butting the agent, and glances back at Anna. "Run."

Anna spins and sprints. *Where?* She rounds the side of the Hummer, throws open its door, slides into the front seat, and reaches for the ignition, hoping like hell that the keys are there. They are. She forces them, igniting the engine, and slams her foot down on the gas pedal. The Hummer shoots forward, away from the spaceship. Agent Glenn's small frame shrinks in the side mirror. She raises a gun.

An intercom clicks on. Mr. Pierson's voice comes through, "Don't shoot."

The agent disappears in the mirror and melts into the frame of the humongous launchpad site. Anna has no idea where she is going. She turns right and hits something—someone. They scream as the Hummer bounces over their body. *Shit.* Headlights rush up behind her, speeding closer. The perimeter gate is still a good distance away. Anna stomps the gas pedal all the way down. The vehicle shoots faster. She twists the steering wheel an inch and the whole damn Hummer tilts on two tires. *Sh …* Anna yanks the wheel the opposite direction. The two tires slam back down. *Shit.* Her ass slides halfway to the passenger seat. She tugs herself back behind the wheel.

The perimeter gate—a three-story brick wall—towers 20 feet ahead. It doesn't matter what is beyond. It is a chance, a different future from where Anna is. Any distance between James' fucked up dad and her is a good thing.

A siren sounds. Red lights spin atop the gate's observation tower. Spikes pop up out of the road, piercing the tires. The Hummer jerks from side to side as the rubber scrapes down to the rims, skidding through the gate, stopping.

There is nothing beyond—nothing but desert in every direction. Two silhouettes appear out of the abyss in front of her.

"I didn't think you had it in you," says Mr. Pierson. He pushes James forward into the headlight's glow, holding a gun to his chin. "But here you are. You see, every step I'm ahead of you. Do you think I didn't see this apocalypse coming?"

A Hummer races up behind Anna, skidding to a stop. Agent Sam hops out, gun drawn. She stops three feet behind Anna and cocks the weapon, pointing it at the back of Anna's head.

"Where's the old lady?" says Mr. Pierson.

"She's being processed," says Sam.

Processed? Anna glances back at the agent, expecting her to say more.

Pierson whacks Anna in the back of the head, sending her spinning. The launchpad and fortification blur.

Anna hits the ground.

Agent Sam pulls out a pair of handcuffs and bends down to handcuff Anna.

"No," yells James, knocking Mr. Pierson out of the way and ramming his shoulder into Agent Sam's.

They fall.

Anna rolls. All the cerebrospinal fluid in her head shifts, sending the pounding sensation to the opposite side of her head. She jumps to her feet, nausea pins her hands to her knees. She shakes it—tries to clear her mind. A Hummer catches her eye. It sits beyond the stretch of headlight. She runs for it.

Shots from the tower rain down behind her, spraying the sand.

Pierson hollers, "Stop!"

They cease fire.

Why? Why make them stop? Anna wants to glance back, see what has happened to James, but if she does, she could fall. She has to look back.

Agent Sam presses a gun against James' back, forcing him into the compound.

Pierson waves to the shooters in the tower. "Take her out!"

Anna focuses on the darkest part of the desert before her, forces her heels into the sand, digging deep footprints into the earth.

A shot rushes through the air, piercing and tearing through her right shoulder. She goes down, face first into the dirt. *Fuck. It burns.* She rolls, trying to expel the shooting pain away. Sand cakes the blood draining out of the wound. Her stomach cramps. *Oh, my God, I'm going to barf.* She moans, rolls—nothing will ease the pain.

Pierson walks up, standing over her.

She wants to grab the fucker's ankle, knock him to the ground and beat the living shit out of him. But she can't move. The pain spreads from the wound. The blood drains away from the tips of her fingers, leaving them numb.

"Get up," he reaches down, "you pathetic piece of trash."

Anna lets out a laugh. She is on the ground bleeding, at the bottom of his feet, and still easy to dehumanize.

He yanks her off the ground.

The gravity shift changes her body's blood flow. It rushes to her shoulder. *Fuck.* She leans an arm toward the ground, trying to ease the pounding in her veins, then falls over.

He doesn't like that. He kicks her, grabs the waist of her jeans, and jerks her to stand. His fat fingers dig across the missing patches of hair and grab hold of what is left, forcing her to follow James' fate.

At least she isn't bent over a park bench.

SPIDER WOMAN

ANNA HAD DRIVEN A LONG WAY TO GET TO THE GATES, much longer than it had seemed. It is a long walk back—way too damn long. Mr. Pierson could've ordered someone to drive them, but he is getting pleasure from forcing Anna to walk the distance.

She feels lightheaded. The bright lights dull to faint blurred lines—a dark world full of glowing balls. The balls dance. Her head begins to weigh ... so heavy. She tilts it to the side, expecting relief—getting a rush of gravity that pushes until she falls over, five feet away from the tower's entrance. A headache pounds through her brain. She rolls enough to flatten her back against the dirt. Above her are two massive black holes—the rockets of a spaceship. At any second they could flick on and swallow her whole, incinerating her.

"Take her to Med Dock," says Pierson. "I'll be up in a few."

The doors swoosh open, but Anna doesn't bother to look at them. James is already long gone. It feels like hours since Agent Sam forced him down the path in front of her.

Pierson's footsteps fade away, deeper into the tower.

Anna stares into the abyss of her fate, the deep funnel of the rockets that will take her away from Earth. It will take her the farthest she can get from the trailer park—from home.

Two agents scoop her up.

She doesn't want to move. Every movement hurts. Her head is going to explode. They drop her on a gurney, undo the handcuffs, and lock them to its guardrail. The gurney jerks forward through the threshold. The world spins. Fluorescent lights race by on the ceiling, like lines on a highway. This building is different from the office one. The gurney stops. Anna's body slides a foot.

A man wearing a lab coat leans into view. "What the hell...?"

"She's all yours, Anderson," says the agent, walking away.

Anderson leans down, his eyes only scratching the surface of all Anna has been through. They linger on the gunshot wound. He leans out of sight, letting the light blind her. The gurney jerks as it moves through a doorway into a large operating room.

There is a sound of air bubbles in water—like there is a huge fish tank hugging the right side of the room, echoing off the walls.

Anderson fumbles with a medical tray and wheels a seat over. His eyes are dark, warm. He is older than Anna, in his 20s maybe—the age where he has to worry about what car he drives, how much rent he has to pay, all the things that really don't matter. Not anymore. Pierson bought him—owned him in the most basic way, and this guy can't even see it, will never see it.

Anna rolls her head away from him, toward the sound of the bubbles. She doesn't want to know what they are going to do to her. She just wants it to be—

Large tubes of white water line the wall. Ms. Murphy's naked, wrinkled body floats inside one. A hose from the top of the tube runs down into her throat. Strands of grey hair float like seaweed, brushing against the glass. Another lab guy stands beside the tube, tapping at its keypad.

What the fuck? Anna squirms, rolls away from Anderson, trying to get off the gurney. He cuffs her other hand. The metal digs into her wrists as she twists and yanks to get out. *Shit.* She kicks her feet, trying to rock herself up. A leather strap restrains her thighs.

"Relax," says Anderson, holding up a scalpel.

Relax? Anna yanks against the cuffs. If she tries hard enough, she can get out. *Fuck this.* She presses her lips together and clenches her eyes, pulling like all hell against the restraints. The handcuffs clink against the gurney's metal. It is no use.

"If you don't relax," says Anderson, "I'll have to knock your ass out."

Did he really just fucking say that to me? Anna stops fighting and opens her eyes.

He simpers.

She rests her head back, staring at the light above. It is no use. She rolls her head, glancing at her future—at the tubes. The lab rat typing on the keypad never lifts his head. He guards Ms. Murphy's swimming corpse. On the other side of him is another tube filled with white liquid. A naked man is inside, butt facing out.

Anderson cuts the shirt around Anna's gunshot wound and peels off the fabric. She can feel the weight of his eyes on her, analyzing every movement, waiting for her to explain why she is here, messing up his lab. *Fuck him.* She isn't in the mood for small talk.

He grabs a bottle of liquid and pours it over her shoulder, into the bullet hole.

It burns. *Fuck.* She screams, trying to sit up, trying to wiggle that shit out of the hole in her shoulder.

He grabs another solution and pours it in.

The pain eases. She lays back down, making damn sure not to look at him, staring at the bright light above her.

"Gibbs," says Anderson.

Lab-rat hurries over from the tubes.

Anderson rolls back, away from Anna.

Gibbs stares at Anna's chest. He's a younger guy, an apprentice maybe. His eyeglasses remind Anna of Jackrabbit.

Jack. The college kid who gave his life for Anna at the colonoscopy.

Gibbs' mouth drops open. "Shit."

Anderson's expression mirrors Gibbs. He too stares at Anna's chest. The liquid from the bullet hole has soaked the collar of her shirt, spreading to the tattoo—now visible beneath the tee-shirt.

Gibbs' eyes shoot back at the tubes—to Ms. Murphy—and return to Anna.

She lays perfectly still on the gurney, relaxed, and closes her eyes. There is nothing she can do, nothing that will change anything.

Gibbs sticks a needle in her arm, draws some blood, and runs it through a machine.

The machine beeps.

His expression drains. He grabs the printout and shows Anderson, saying, "Can we…?"

"Let me patch her up first," says Anderson, wheeling back to

Anna's side. He pulls out a curved needle and thread. "Get me the Bloodwort."

Bloodwort? Chills shoot through Anna's veins and she pulls her head up, trying to see where Gibbs is going. *That's it. The word. The Native.*

He walks past the wall of tubes, to the back of the room, and presses his hand against a flat wall. The blue metal panels slide open like a door. Shelves filled with dry herbs, encased in glass containers, are lit by a warm light.

Anderson shoves the needle into Anna's shoulder and pulls the string through.

It burns. *Oh, God.* She lays her head back, clenching her teeth, sucking in a long, hard breath.

He stitches the strings through her flesh, one after another.

"Should we shave her before you stitch the exit hole?" Gibbs says, coming back over.

An alarm sounds through the intercom. A woman's voice announces, "Two hours before departure."

"How many more to process?" says Anderson.

"Just the McAllisters." Gibbs holds out a glass jar full of dried leaves.

Anderson pulls and knots the last stitch, glancing at the herb jar. "Good. Mix it."

Gibbs disappears behind Anderson.

A metal bowl hits the counter, spinning like a saucer.

"Do you have your period?" says Anderson.

What? Blush fills Anna's cheeks, bringing her attention to the cold ventilation. *That's none of your goddamn business.*

"I don't want to be surprised." He slaps on a surgical mask and gloves.

What the fuck? "What are you doing?"

"Calm down," he says, grabbing a scalpel. "I don't want to cut you."

Her heart pounds, cutting off the air from her lungs. He walks to the foot of the gurney. Anna lifts her head to see what the fuck he is doing.

"I'm taking off the patient's pants," he says.

"Like hell you are," she says. It is bad enough Anna is strapped to a table. There is no way she is going to be molested. *Fuck this.* She clenches her fists, digging her nails into her palms, fighting the handcuffs.

"Gibbs…" says Anderson.

Lab-rat runs over and stabs her in the arm with something.

Everything goes limp. Her head falls back. Her fingers roll open. She can move her eyes, but she cannot move anything else. *I can't move!*

"Relax," says Anderson. "We're not going to hurt you."

What the fuck does he call this?

He touches her leg.

She can feel the pressure of his hand, but can't *feel* it. She can't move. Tears ball in the corners of her eyes, but she can't blink to free them. She can't swallow.

The pressure of his hand moves to the leather strap over her body, pulling it off. The sound of fabric ripping should send shockwaves up Anna's spine, but everything is too numb. Anderson holds his hand out above her. "Razor."

Gibbs grabs something from the surgical tray behind Anna and hands it over.

"Well," says Anderson, his eyes plastered to Anna's vagina. He flicks on an electric razor. "I see you didn't leave much work for me."

What are you doing? Anna can't scream. She can't demand answers. *I can't fucking move.*

"We can't risk an outbreak of crabs." The buzz of the razor moves toward her body, deepening in vibration against skin she cannot feel. "The oxygen solution kills everything else."

She watches Ms. Murphy float in the liquid tube across the room as Anderson shaves the hair between her legs.

"There," he says. The hum of the razor ceases. "That wasn't so bad, huh?"

The guy beside Ms. Murphy spins in the liquid. His shaved penis is followed by a set of abs and tight arms. Thick dreadlocks of hair float in the white substance. His eyes are wide open, unmoving.

James.

"Warm blanket," Anderson says over his shoulder. "And you can start measuring her trachea."

Gibbs leans down into Anna's view, blocking the wall of tubes. He pushes his glasses on better and grabs Anna's cheeks, straightening her head, forcing her eyes back to the ceiling. He sticks the end of a ruler against her bottom lip, pushing her lips apart.

She tries to close her mouth, but it doesn't work. She is trapped, paralyzed.

He trades the ruler for a large circle, holding it to her lips. Too small. He tries another. Too small. He tries another and lets out a breath of relief. He swaps the ring for a tube, setting it alongside her on the gurney.

He's going to shove it down my throat. No. They can't put her in one of those things. *No. It'll fill to the top—I'll drown. I can't breathe.*

The doors swoosh open.

Mr. Pierson enters, letting out a moan. "The McAllisters are here. Make it quick. Anderson, prep them. Gibbs, finish this one up."

"It takes two to flip her," says Anderson.

"Go." Pierson nods at him. "I'll help Gibbs."

No. Anna doesn't want him anywhere near her.

Pierson's breathing deepens as he leans over the gurney, sticking a key in the cuffs and grabbing hold of Anna's wrist. "I see the dragonfly." He tosses the keys to Gibbs, who unlocks the other handcuff. Pierson's fingers slide down her stomach, stopping at the tip of shaved hair.

No.

His fingertips slide to her hip, and he rolls her toward Gibbs, facing her away from the tubes.

"Give us a minute," says Pierson, tightening the cuffs to the gurney rails.

Fuck.

Gibbs hesitates and then walks away. The lab doors swoosh open and shut with his departure, leaving them alone.

A ball catches in Anna's throat. The pounding of her breath against the gurney overpowers the sound of the bubbling tubes.

Pierson's fingers grab the ruler off the gurney and whack Anna's ass with it. The impact shakes her body enough to make her breasts press into the mattress. His breathing intensifies. "You like disobeying me?"

Fuck you.

He swings the ruler again and her body quivers with the impact. "Do you?" He hits her again and again.

She won't be able to sit down later. But he'll pay. She'll make him pay.

The door swooshes open.

She can't see anything but the medical tray and rolling chair. It is quiet. Whoever came in hasn't said anything. Pierson exhales with loss of breath. He drops the ruler, smacks her ass with an open palm, and digs his fingers into the side of her thigh.

It isn't the first time a guy ran his disgusting fingers between her legs. She can't feel it, but the memory begins sketching itself into Anna's storyline. She wants to close her eyes, pretend it isn't happening.

"Mr. Pierson ..." Gibbs says in a low voice.

The doors swoosh shut behind him.

Pierson clears his throat and the pressure of his fingers pull away from Anna's skin. His shoes tap as he rounds the table and leans down. She doesn't want to see his fucking face, but there is no choice. He has taken her free will. Beads of sweat cling to the pores of his upper lip. Sewage leaches out of his mouth with the words, "Sweet dreams on the flight out."

Anna looks away. She would do anything to get away from his cesspool of a soul.

His fingers grab her cheeks, forcing her eyes back to his. "When we get there, you're going to know what pain is." Pierson redirects his attention to Gibbs. "Hurry up." His grip deepens, pinching Anna's cheeks together. His greasy lips press against hers. The beads of sweat on his lips smear across her skin. She can't close her eyes to pretend it isn't happening. He stares at her as he kisses her harder, then pulls away, and pushes her face down against the table. "I'm going to make sure you're just like this when I fuck you."

He walks away. She can't see him, but she can hear that fat fucker's feet stomping toward the doors.

They swoosh open and close.

Medical instruments clink behind Anna with Gibbs' movement. A Bunsen burner clicks on. A glass lid slides onto the counter.

The doors swoosh open with Anderson's return. Anna's heart should have jumped, but instead it rhythmically slows.

His voice raises, "You haven't sewn her up yet?" His words

slow as he gets closer. "What the fuck is this?"

"Seems our boss is a bit of a sadist," says Gibbs.

"Jesus," says Anderson, sitting down, rolling closer. He looks at Anna's face, avoiding her eyes. "Let's stitch you up, okay?"

She can't nod. She can't swallow or wipe the taste of the asshole's mouth from her lips—pull her goddamn pants up.

Anderson digs the needle into the back of her shoulder and sews the edges of flesh together, tugging like a corset.

Gibbs approaches, cupping a steaming mug. His hands shake. "Are you sure about this?"

Anderson grunts an "uh-huh." He cuts the stitching thread and sets the items down. "She'll die if we don't."

Die? The word should have surprised Anna, but she knew it —felt it—for three years, since that spring morning.

A thunderstorm woke her. Anna's stomach cramped. It wasn't her usual premenstrual pain. That arrived a week prior. She used the bathroom and wiped. There was blood on the toilet paper. It was the first day there was blood on the toilet paper. Dr. Mullins' face said it all a week ago. Preliminary tests confirmed Anna is dying. Maybe more tests were the only thing Dr. Mullins needed to build up the courage to tell her.

Anderson leans closer. "Why would you think you can't turn the tonic in your veins into water?"

The building begins to rumble—vibrate. The spaceship engines kick on, warming up to shoot them all off this dying planet.

I can't… It's impossible. Anna focuses on her limp hand, trying to wiggle her pinky.

Nothing.

He leans closer. "Or that the restraints could keep you down?"

It is impossible, yet Anna's pinky twitches. She stares into his eyes and envisions moving her hand. *It works.* She bends her wrist, barely touching the handcuff. It explodes into water molecules. She rolls off the table, away from them.

The sheets are soaked in water where the handcuff once hung. It isn't supposed to be possible.

Both lab-techs stare at the spot with their mouths gaping open.

Anna can't believe it. She stretches her fingers out to the throat tube, laying on a nearby medical tray. They shake. She has to see it. She has to see it disappear.

"Concentrate," says Gibbs. His weight shifts and he steps closer.

Anna angles the gurney, barricading him from her.

Steam rises from the mug in his hands while he stays put.

The blurred lines of the gurney strap crisp in Anna's view. The curves of her fingerprints run across the fibers of the leather strap. The molecules shift, and the strap bursts like a water balloon. *Shit.*

Gibbs steps closer, holding out the mug. "It's much harder not turning things."

Anna still can't believe it. She shoves her palms down against the gurney.

Gibbs takes another step closer. "Water," rolls off his lips.

It repeats in Anna's head, *Water.*

The gurney explodes all over them. Drops of water descend from the ceiling, like those left in a tree after a thunderstorm.

She grabs the mug. Inside, black tea dimples from the spacecraft-rocket's vibration. It begins to stabilize.

"Hurry," says Gibbs. "Drink it."

"You can't change things back," says Anderson.

If they want to kill me, poison is a shitty way to do it. She downs the tea. Nothing happens. "It didn't do anything."

Anderson smiles.

The room spins. Anna twists around, looking for something to hold onto. *James.* He floats in the white liquid behind her. She leans her head against his tube, staring at Ms. Murphy. The black dragonfly appears blue beneath the white liquid— swimming—drowning in it. She presses her palm against James' tube.

"No!" yell the men.

The glass pops. White liquid pours out, knocking Anna down. James' body floods out, bumping her feet, half in the tube, face down.

Anderson grabs Anna's wrists, forcing them behind her back. She is not going to be restrained again. She swings back her head, slamming it into his. He lets go, moaning.

Gibbs runs over to Ms. Murphy, pinning his back against her tube, guarding her.

Anna stands, dripping in the solution that will carry her to another world—a life she doesn't want—a life too far from home.

James moans and rolls onto his side.

Anna grabs the tube sticking out of his mouth, and pulls it out.

He throws up all over the place, looking up like an abused, wet cat. His lungs heave the air in and out of them, gasping.

Anna glances back at Ms. Murphy.

Gibbs holds his hands up in defense.

"Anna!" says Anderson.

What have they done for me? Given me the freedom I deserved? Fuck that. She stands up and goes for her.

"No." Gibbs takes a swing at Anna yelling, "Not her!"

Anna ducks, coming back with an open-palm shove to his forehead. The back of his head whacks the tube and he explodes like a raindrop. *Oh, my God!* She stares at him—the not him. Anderson is going to pummel her. She can feel it.

The lab doors open.

A couple walks in; it is the McAllisters, no doubt. The woman wears a white fur coat. The man, linked to her arm, is in his 40s—half her age. Her eyes land on Anna. Her body jerks to a stop while her long, diamond earrings keep swinging. Her white gloves press against ruby-red lips, smearing the lipstick. The man's smile fades.

Shit. Anna scoops an arm beneath James' shoulder, making sure her fingers don't touch him. He is groggy, but leans against her, holding half his weight, taking an accompanying step.

Anderson climbs to his feet behind them, pinching a bleeding nose.

Anna pulls James harder toward the door, running. James' weight shifts as they pass the couple. Anna's bare shoulder bumps into the man's arm and he explodes into a million droplets. The old woman screams.

Oh, my God. It isn't just her hands. Anna's breath stops. She wants to let go, drop James. *He might … he could … pop…* She stops in the corridor. *No! Don't think it.* If she lets go, he won't be safe and she doesn't want to be alone.

"Right." James' scratchy voice interrupts her thoughts. He knows where they are.

Anna turns right.

The hall splits in three directions.

"Left," he says.

Anna heads for a door at the hall's end.

James' weight shifts when they get to it. It doesn't open like the others. He reaches to the right of its door. His fingers brush the blue metal wall and a red keypad glows beneath the surface. It scans his fingerprints.

The door opens to an elevator. Anyone looking for them could find them now. Whatever system allows him access will also be the reason for their demise. Once they step in, there is no getting out, no chance of escape.

Anna pulls him in. They are in no position to outrun anyone. The clock has already started. It is only a matter of time before the entire building is searched for them.

The doors close and the capsule shoots up, spilling them out onto a loading dock several stories above. It looks like a warehouse, except the blue metal gives an illusion that everything is sterile. The walls reach three-stories high and keep going, lined with rows of tubes.

What the fuck? Ten feet in front of them are bodies—tubes of bodies lined up like soldiers—waiting to be filed away.

The sound of a forklift zooms closer. Its headlights rush faster, grow larger in the depth of the loading dock.

The heart palpitations from impending doom subside, in lieu of awe at the rows of people. There are so many. So many who had entrusted strangers to bottle them up and ship them off to another world. They sleep, leaving the Earth to die, believing some white solution will protect them until the next world.

James grabs Anna's hand and dashes behind the tubes, hiding.

The forklift comes closer, squeaking to a halt. Someone whistles a tune—something from when Anna was little.

James lets go of Anna's hand and steps out from behind the tubes. "I know that song anywhere."

A guy in his late 20s jumps off the forklift, adjusting the ballcap on his head. "Jesus, James. You scared the shit out of ..." he steps closer, noticing James' dripping wet, naked body. "He tried, huh?"

James tugs Anna out into the open—completely naked, shaved and all.

His friend's eyes dart to the dragonfly tattoo. "James?"

"Yeah," James says. "I know."

The elevator opens behind them.

The guy's reaction gets stuck in his throat. He darts toward Anna, grabs her hand, and drags her toward the forklift.

"James?" she says.

"Go," he says, releasing her hand.

A wall of agents storms out of the elevator.

James' friend pulls her into the forklift and takes off, deeper into the spaceship's warehouse bay. He jerks the wheel this way and that. "Hey! I'm Cliff. You're...?"

James lets out a cry of agony as an agent tasers him. He falls to his knees. A different agent punches him to the floor.

"Hold on!" Cliff swerves the forklift to the right and then the left. He cuts the wheel so tight that he has to go the opposite direction to rebalance the forklift. "I guess you're the Dragonfly."

"I'm Anna." The words surprise her. She had never cared for the name—it was basic, as common as any other. She isn't some dragonfly—some mystical insect.

He pulls over. "Get out."

What?

"I'll come back for you." He glances over his shoulder. "Get out!"

She hops off and he peels away.

Headlights come up from behind, in the distance.

Shit. Anna slides in between two tubes. Thank God she's flat-chested. If her boobs were any bigger, she wouldn't have fit.

Three Hummers shoot by. Their tires squeal in the distance. Deep voices command answers from Cliff.

Anna leans her head against a tube, waiting for the pounding in her heart to ease.

An old lady floats in white solution, bumping up against the glass. Black strands of hair intertwine into a long, thick braid of white hair, creating a spider web pattern.

I can break her out.

The glass pops beneath Anna's fingers. The white liquid pours against her body. *Shit.*

The old woman's body falls into her arms.

A stampede of guards comes for them. The headlights of a Hummer head back their way.

The old woman moans.

Anna just ruined her life. *Who is she?* Everything about her reminds Anna of the Indian in the café.

Her eyes open, widening with fear at the tube protruding from her throat.

Anna pulls it out.

The woman hacks up some of the white solution. Her natural breasts sag into cones, swinging against her ribs. She points up toward Anna with a crooked finger, tapping against the dragonfly on her chest. Then points at herself. No words come out.

A Hummer skids to a stop beside them. Agent Sam jumps out.

The old woman tries to speak again. Raspy sounds form into the words, "Spider … Spider Woman."

Transporter

Like a dragonfly trapped in a spider web, Agent Sam tasers Anna. The next time Anna opens her eyes, it is pitch black. The hum of tires coasting beneath a vehicle indicates that she is back in the Hummer. *Not again*.

A guy moans in the darkness.

"Who's there?" she says.

He moans again.

James? She waits for an answer, but only another moan comes. Silence takes over. The pitch-black space shrinks in the stillness. "Where are they taking us?"

"The Transporter," says Cliff, coughing.

Anna eases a little, knowing who is with her, even if she is cold, naked, and locked inside some box with a strange man. So far, he seems like a nice guy and she could take him if needed. Easily. What scares her is where they are going.

Her hands are bound in front of her this time. She presses her fingers against the handcuffs. *Water.* Nothing happens. *Water.* Nothing. *Not now.* Out of all the times, possibilities, it has to be now—when she needs it the most—that she can't use it. She closes her eyes in the dark and pictures a waterfall shooting down the side of a mountain. Snowflakes sprinkle from a moonlit sky.

A deep rumble explodes outside, vibrating the Hummer.

Anna pulls her legs in, trying to protect herself from whatever it is. "What's that?"

"It..." comes a woman's soft, gentle voice, "is the last ship off this planet."

"No," Cliff's voice trembles. "There's one more."

"I can't go." The words come out of Anna so quickly, she hardly recognizes her voice. Ms. Murphy told her she had to stay. She doesn't know why—and she doesn't care. She doesn't have any want to leave earth, to drown with no oxygen in a tank of white liquid. "You have to help me. I can't leave Earth."

It is quiet. The humming tires torment Anna with the silence.

"At least it's a free ticket," Cliff says. "You have any idea how lucky we are? Do you know how much tickets for the Oasis cost?"

Lucky? Anna doesn't feel lucky. The old woman with spider-weaved hair sitting across from her, had chosen to go. Anna took that from her. The old woman now sits soaking wet, with strangers—because of Anna. She asks her, "What'd you pay?"

"It isn't about the money," says Spider Woman. "It's about being there to protect the next planet we find. There is no price for that."

"Starting price," says Cliff, "is three million dollars. The more you pay, the more you're guaranteed a spot as council in the new world."

A new world? They destroyed this one: greed, control, fear of being ordinary. They destroyed so many lives. It was so easy for them to leave, to put themselves first, before all the rest of humanity. Anna had so many questions. Was it so bad that Earth had to be abandoned? Couldn't a vaccine be found? Couldn't they turn things around? Wait it out? An image of James pops into her head. She looks at Cliff. "Why doesn't he want to go?"

"He's not ready to give up on her," says Cliff.

Her? Anna's heart sinks. *I knew it, he's with someone.* There is always someone else. Always. "Who?"

"Earth."

Anna's heart should've eased, but it tightened. There were signs: the dry summers, the warmer winters, the increase of Californians in town. Even the blind could feel the planet dying. Humanity let year after year fade away, not doing anything to save her, or themselves. You can taste it in the water, see it in the oil staining our oceans, breathe it in the morning dew. A mass extinction was already underfoot. Humanity deserved it. Humans already caused the extinction of so many species on the planet. It is only right for it to be their turn.

"What about you?" Anna says to Cliff. "What were you going to do? Leave? Be a slave for the rich?"

"At least I wouldn't die here." Cliff's voice turns soft and cracks with the words, "I'd have a chance there, get to see the stars, be amongst legends …"

"You already are," Spider Woman says.

Cliff coughs, muffling it in the bend of his arm. When he is done, he lets out a chuckle like the old lady is crazy.

The wheels move faster beneath the Hummer, weaving here and there. It runs over something. The tires screech to a halt. Anna slides across the floor and her naked body smashes against something else—someone sweaty.

Cliff coughs. His breath blows against her neck.

Shit. She pushes away him and scoots backward until her back is pressed up against the back doors.

"Isn't it funny?" says the old woman. "We live our whole life crossing paths with people, never really knowing them. Every day our lives collide and we never see them as they are. We see their clothes, their hairstyles, the garden boxes outside their trailers. But we never see them—as they are—naked."

Goosebumps crawl over Anna's skin. *How does she know about the garden boxes?*

"Strangers," she says, "leave us clues as to where we should be going. And we choose to follow them or not."

Cliff hacks up another cough that can't be contained.

"We can see everything coming." She raises her voice over his noise. "If only we stop rushing through our lives long enough."

No. Anna refuses to believe that. Her parents are dead. There wasn't anything that could've warned her, nothing she could've done to change anything. No amount of time she could have slowed to save them.

"Sometimes we ignore things so deeply, life has a way of waking us up. Like a slap in the face, a tearing of the heart, a spirit animal, an old man ordering tea."

Oh, my God. How? No. She can't know that. But she does. "How...?"

"All it takes is one person. One person to change things, fix things, finish things."

"I don't know what I'm supposed to do!" Anna yells. *I don't lump what I'm supposed to do.*

The cabin falls quiet.

Cliff breaths heavy.

The chill of the cold metal penetrates Anna's body and the conversation isn't helping any. Spider Woman doesn't say anything else. Anna wants to demand more from her. But what is she going to ask after all of that? Her heart pounds. She eases the words, "What should I do?"

The Native from the café pops into her mind's eye. His eyes glow and he morphs into the owl perched on Meagan's shed. *The napkin.* It wipes away all concentration she had on the owl.

Her thoughts crisp with the image of the napkin. The shaky writing on it spells Bloodwort. The white color of the napkin fades into the image and memory of a doctor's lab coat. Gibbs is offering the tea to her. *What am I supposed to do? Why me? Why the fuck won't she just tell me?* Gibbs' face morphs into the crackhead from the park. Anna's heart jumps and her eyes open to a dark room. *It was all fate? All meant to guide me through this goddamn shitty life? Bullshit.*

All she wants is to be back home in the trailer with Mom. She wants to laugh with Jeremy again. She wants to tell Megan she doesn't really believe she is a whore. She doesn't want to be naked in the back of a vehicle with people who don't mean shit to her. She doesn't want them all to be dead. But they are.

The vehicle stops. The back doors open, letting in moonlight.

Dr. Anderson and Agent Sam guard the exit. They are back at the office.

What the fuck?

Cliff has another coughing fit.

"Shit, Cliff," says Anderson. "You look like hell."

"At least I don't have your ugly face," says Cliff.

Anderson puckers his lips and bites his tongue.

Agent Sam whips out a baton, cracking it to its full length. "Get out."

"Let's go," Anderson says, grabbing Anna's arm. "We've got a spaceship to dock with before the Oasis sets off for E2."

UNBOUND

LIKE HELL.

In reality, there is nothing Anna can do, not with her hands bound. She looks up at the ship, following its curved metal to the night not yet washed out by the sun.

Spider Woman and Cliff follow Anderson into the building.

Agent Sam steps closer.

There is no way Anna can take her. She slides out of the Hummer and does as she is supposed to. She keeps her eyes to the left, anticipating a screaming woman to pop out of nowhere, like before.

The doors open.

Anna digs her heels into the floor until she see him.

James stands in the middle of the lobby wearing a tuxedo.

"What is this?" Anna says, ready to storm him.

Agent Sam grabs Anna's arm.

Anna shakes her off and charges him. "You sold me out!"

He nods at the agent. She slaps Anna, knocking her to the ground.

Fuck. Anna's cheek throbs. She drags herself to stand, pressing her fingertips against the handcuff's metal, concentrating. *Water.*

Nothing happens.

She notices the cuff's metal has a slight blue tint to it. *Water. Water.* She presses her fingers harder. *Come on….*

"It won't work," says Anderson, before he disappears behind the receptionist's desk.

"Why not?" asks Anna.

James nods at Sam. She backs off of Anna. He walks over, sliding his fingers along her arm to the cuffs, so close she can feel his suit press against her chest as he inhales.

Forcefully, Sam makes herself known in the corner of Anna's vision, crossing her arms in discontent.

"Leave us," he says to her, staring into Anna's eyes.

"I'm sorry," Agent Sam says, "but that is against orders."

He faces her, withdrawing his fingers from Anna's skin. "Sam, I'm not going to play your games. I am in charge here."

Sam pulls the sword from her belt, takes a step toward him, pressing the tip of her nose against his. "You can tell them whatever you want. And you can think whatever you want. But you are not in charge here."

He smiles, steps back, pulls Anna into his arms, and presses his lips against hers.

Sam makes a low growl and storms down the corridor after Anderson.

Anna is ready for answers. She nudges him away, turning enough to reach the handcuffs out to him. "Un-cuff me."

"I think I like you like this," he says.

Her heart jumps. Her cheeks warm. *Is he serious?* She can't tell if he is flirting, or if something is seriously fucked up with him. "You think Billionaire-businessman does it for me?"

He pulls away, straightens his jacket, and nods toward the corridor. "Go, Anna."

Guess he didn't like that. Her cheeks burn with embarrassment. She walks past him into the dark hallway. A light penetrates the corridor from the left.

Inside, it looks like the other laboratory, except much smaller. Four gurneys line the right side. Cliff lays on the back one, looking like shit. There is a dark room that sits off to his side.

Spider Woman has pulled on a hospital gown and taken the second gurney, one away from Cliff.

Agent Sam stands beside the door. A shitty grin smears

across her lips when she sees Anna. She dumps a hospital gown in Anna's arms and shoves her toward the first gurney.

Anderson loads an operating tray across from Anna, going on and on about E2—Earth Two. The transporter will shoot them into space, dock with Oasis, and carry them away from the only planet Anna has ever known.

"Don't leave," Ms. Murphy's voice shoots through Anna's thoughts, muffling all the technical details of how they will be "processed" for the journey.

Cliff starts coughing. He rolls to his side, hunched in a fetal position with his back to them.

Anderson runs over to him.

Sam joins him, grabbing Cliff's gurney, then pushes him into the side room. "We need to scan him." Her voice muffles like she has put on a mask. "I can't have you contaminating the whole damn mission."

He restrains a cough. "I'm fine."

James walks in, throwing his jacket on the chair behind Anna, and starts to unbutton his shirt.

"You sold me out," she says.

He looks at her, letting his eyes take in the curves of her body. He takes a step, spreading her knees to draw himself closer.

Her heart races. Blood floods into her cheeks, blushing them. She pleads, "You've got to get me out of here."

His fingers brush a piece of hair from her cheek. "You could be a god on E2."

"I don't want to be a god."

"Maybe it's time to give up, give in." He takes the hospital gown from her, sliding it over her head.

"Dragonfly..." says Spider Woman from the gurney behind Anna.

Jesus. Anna forgot she was there.

Anderson screams.

Anna pushes James away and jumps off the gurney. He grabs the handcuffs and unlocks them.

Anderson runs out of the backroom, pressing his hand up against his ear. Blood seeps between his fingers. Cliff follows, snarling. He grabs hold of Anderson's lab coat, yanking him back—to the ground—and bites Anderson's hand, chomping down on his fingers. Sam follows with her sword drawn and swings down, chopping off Cliff's arm. He doesn't scream. His eyes shift to her. She swings again, slicing off his head. Anderson looks at his missing fingers, the blood oozing from their nubs, and cries.

Agent Sam swings the blade back over her head and stares down at him.

"What are you doing?" he says through thick sobs.

"I'm sorry," she says, swinging the blade down.

He shields it with his forearms and ducks his head. The blade slices through it all.

Anna turns away. Her stomach knots and retches.

"Shit," says James.

Anna holds onto the gurney, forcing her stomach acid back

down, looking back at Anderson's bloody—

Oh, God, I can't.

Agent Sam looks at James and points the blade at him. "You."

He steps back.

"You fix this," she says, pointing the sword at Anderson's corpse and back at James.

He lifts his hands in defense.

"I know you know how to process tubes." She steps over Anderson and makes for James.

He backs up. The doors swoosh open. Miscalculation leaves his back pinned up against the edge of the threshold.

Agent Sam gets closer, lowers her sword, pulls out a gun and aims at his heart. "Now."

He looks into her eyes. "No."

She steps closer, pressing the pistol against his cheek. "Now!"

This is it. Anna takes a swing at her. Agent Sam catches her hand mid-air, twists it, forces Anna to her knees, and presses the barrel of the gun to the back of her head.

Spider Woman whales Sam from behind with the medical tray. The agent loses balance. The gun falls away from Anna's skin, skids across the floor, and stops at James' feet.

He picks it up.

Sam moans, holding the back of her head, looking at the old woman, saying, "You stupid—"

Spider Woman swings the tray again, flattening her to the ground, knocking her the fuck out.

James stands, staring at her limp body. The gun shakes at his side.

"Hey," Anna says.

He doesn't move.

"James!" she says.

His eyes drift and meet Anna's, but he isn't all there. He looks back at Sam and aims the gun at her.

Spider Woman walks up to him and slides her fingers onto his shoulder, staring past him, nodding in approval.

The gun goes off.

Sam's body shakes with the bullet's impact and a line of blood leaks out from beneath her.

Spider Woman's fingers slide down his arm, taking away the gun. "There."

He sinks to the floor, burying his face in his hands.

She sits, wrapping her arms around him. "There, there."

Anna can't stand there anymore. She has to get out of there. *I need to get these handcuffs off.* She glances down at Sam's lifeless body. *Fuck that.* No way is Anna frisking a corpse in search of handcuff keys. She paces and the room blurs. *Where ... what...?* She can't make sense of anything, wrap her brain around anything solid. The blue metal cabinets beneath the far counter gleam with the light's reflection. Anna throws open their doors, one after another.

No key. Nothing—nothing but medical supplies, bandages, weird plastic tubes and clamps, needles, paper gowns, and an electric shaver.

She grabs a handful of hospital gowns and throws them to the floor, looking back at Agent Sam's lifeless corpse. She stands, knowing that she will have to slide her fingers down into the agent's pockets, feel the last of her warmth fade away.

James quiets down, keeping his head buried. Spider Woman watches Anna from his side.

Anna bends down beside Agent Sam. The color in her cheeks has faded. There is no telling if she is infected. Anna has no fucking idea how ... what is causing ... people to kill each other. She focuses on Sam's front pocket: the stitching, the intermittent lines like those running down a road. Anna slides her fingers into the fabric, watching it come to life as her fingers wiggle inside.

Nothing. There is no fucking key.

She yanks her hand out—away from the dead body. There is a second pocket. *I can't do this.* Anna has to stand and step over the corpse to get to the other side, to maneuver the handcuffs the right way. She heaves the fear from her lungs and stands, kneeling on her other side.

How long were we in the back of the Hummer with Cliff? If it was a virus, was it airborne? The saliva in Anna's mouth thickens. She looks down at Sam.

She knew. Anna would put money on it that Sam knew exactly what is wrong with the world.

James. Anna looks at him.

He sucks up his tears and stands.

The puddle of blood beneath Sam expands.

Anna can't I do it—stick her fingers down against Sam's body again. She tries to focus on the pocket's stitching—the fabric—but it blurs more. Seconds ago, Agent Sam was breathing. Anna draws her eyes away, to the edges of the room.

A small bathroom sits behind her.

She has to get out of here, get away from her—them. They are infected. Anna doesn't want to turn into that—into a monster —a zombie.

She makes for the bathroom and slams the door closed behind her. The walls cave in on her and she falls to her knees, slumping into a heap in the corner.

She stays there for a while. The hum of the lights takes any noise. Spider Woman and James converse outside, but it doesn't matter. It feels good to be alone.

The ventilation kicks on. Cold air blows from a vent above, irritating the missing patches of Anna's hair. She uses the bathroom. Residual methane from her colonoscopy leaks out and her ass feels wet as usual. She wipes. There is blood, but it is a rust color. It is no longer a bright red. Anna wipes again, confirming it. *It's not red.* She finishes cleaning-up and stands.

The mirror captures the worn figure of a beaten and abused woman. Anna hardly recognizes herself. *The razor they'd used to shave me.* She flings open the bathroom door.

James and Spider Woman's conversation ceases mid-sentence.

Anna makes for the cabinets, searching one after another until finding the razor-blade.

They both stare from across the room at her.

She runs back into the bathroom and jams the plug into the outlet.

James approaches from behind. "What are you doing?"

She clicks on the razor.

Spider Woman appears behind James, smirking.

Anna lets their faces fade into the background as she stares at the patches of her hair. A chill crawls up her spine as if the coke-head's hands are restraining hers. *No.* She won't let it cripple her, rip pieces off anymore. She shaves the middle of her scalp, scraping a strip of hair off before she can change her mind.

James' jaw drops and he walks away, disappearing from the frame of the mirror.

Spider Woman leans in the doorway. "You know the dragonfly spends the majority of its life as a nymph."

Anna strips off another row of hair, watching the long pieces fall to the ground. She has never cut her hair before, not once.

Spider Woman steps into the room. "Before they take adult form you never see them, unless you swim below the water."

Anna loses her grip on the razor. It falls into the sink, buzzing and vibrating against the porcelain.

The old woman steps alongside Anna, pulls the razor out of the sink, presses her opposite hand against the back of Anna's head and slides the vibrating metal over her scalp, shedding the rest of her exuviae.

What have I done? The girl in the mirror is no longer me.

"You have to crawl out of the water," Spider Woman leans in, "high up above the lake, to change."

Anna looks at the tattoo on her breast. *What have I done?*

"I warn you."

Anna's heart races. *Oh, no.*

"Metamorphosis can hurt like a bitch." She brushes the last locks of hair from her shoulder. "Embrace it, and it will hurt less."

"What if I don't?" Anna's eyes meet hers in the mirror. *I didn't want to be in this world—a world where I only live in the moment, because that's all there is.*

Spider Woman freezes, staring back at Anna. "Then you will only suffer longer."

"I don't want this life."

She turns off the razor. "Find gratitude. There are so many who no longer breathe, who will never have a chance to climb out above the water."

TANGLED WEB

SPIDER WOMAN LEAVES ANNA ALONE WITH HER reflection.

What have I done? Anna runs her fingers over the stubble of her hair. Shavings cake to the scab patches and torn follicles. She dips her face into the sink, splashing water over it, out of view from the woman in the mirror. At least this way no man is going to grab hold of her hair and force her into anything.

James leans in the doorway. "You ready?"

Anna doesn't have to ask where they are going. They sure as hell aren't making that flight into space. Something about that fact comforts her. She doesn't know what Mr. Pierson plans on doing with Ms. Murphy, but Anna has stayed on Earth as she insisted. Ms. Murphy is destined to be a god while Anna is left in the ashes.

James comes up behind Anna, wrapping his arms around her waist, leaning his chin on her shoulder. She spins in his arms, pressing her chest against his. His thumb brushes her cheek and she lets him kiss her. A flood of energy surges through Anna's veins and she sinks into his arms. She wants to feel the vulnerability, the complete lack of responsibility sex brings. Her fingers run down his back. She pulls them away. *I could've killed him.*

"What?" he asks.

"I don't want to ..." she looks at her hands. "I could kill you."

He reaches for her shoulder, to bring her back closer.

"No." She yanks it away, and looks at the floor, avoiding his eyes. *No.* She looks at the mirror—at a marked woman, a cursed girl. "I'll never be normal."

"Why would you ever want to be?" he asks.

"That's easy for you to say." She pushes past him to get out of the tiny ass bathroom. "You were the rich kid. Weren't you? Probably played varsity lacrosse or some shit."

"You think I fit in with those greedy, self-centered, earth-killing assholes?" His voice rises.

She studies the twists of his dreadlocks, the curves of his muscles etched by excessive hours of surfing, and his feet: barefoot and dirty. She looks into his eyes, to peer into his soul.

Maybe she projected her worthlessness onto him, but she isn't ready to let go of it. His eyes stay still as she searches them. She turns for the door. "Let's go."

Spider Woman is gone.

No. She is supposed to guide Anna through all this. *Shit.* Anna runs out of the lab.

The corridor is empty.

James passes her, sprinting down the hall. "Check the other way."

Anna runs into the lobby. It is dark. *The dragonfly.* She runs to the left office.

The woman is there, sitting at the desk in the dark, neatly stacking papers. She scoops up the broken picture frame, dumps the glass into the trash bin, and leans down to pull a small piece of paper from the bin. "What do you notice when you're in here?"

There is no question, it is the dragonfly.

"Why?" Spider Woman's eyes follow Anna's.

"It's huge," says Anna.

She smiles and chuckles to herself. "Would you notice it if it were small?"

"Yes. It reminds me of the café where I work ... worked."

Spider Woman's eyes narrow.

"This one is bigger, but the other is much more eye-catching. When the sun peeks through the clouds and its rays stretch across the café, its pieces of mirror sparkle."

"La Café?" she says.

How … does she know that?

She holds up the paper from the trash bin—a receipt—and lets it go.

It floats like a feather back into the trash.

"Is there anything special about it?" asks Spider Woman.

"No." There is nothing special. It hangs over a booth situated by the counter, windowless, and …." Soft words come out, "The Native."

Her eyes ease to a normal position and she nods for me to continue.

"He,"Anna reaches for the dragonfly on her chest, "sat there … But that has nothing to do with anything." The image of Ms. Murphy's wrinkled tattoo shoots through Anna's thoughts. She follows the black strains of hair tangled in Spider Woman's long white braid. "I don't understand. Nothing connects…" She looks around the room. There are no clues to what the fuck she is supposed to be doing. *This is crazy. There's nothing here that—*

Spider Woman taps on the picture.

The girl.

The old woman smiles.

"But what does she have to do with me … with this?"

Spider Woman stands up and rests a hand on Anna's shoulder. "Everything."

PHOTOGRAPHS

JAMES POPS HIS HEAD INTO THE OFFICE. "READY?"

Anna stares at the picture. There are two women, but Anna only knows the one Spider Woman refers to—the one with the blond curls, Ms. Perfect, the girl Meadowlark hunts. Anna faces James. "Who is she?"

"What?" he says, leaning in the door.

Spider Woman scoots out of the office.

Anna picks up the picture frame. Light scratches from the broken glass distort the once-perfect memory. "Don't fuck with me, James." She holds out the picture. "This isn't a coincidence."

He takes his time to come up with something. He has two choices: the truth or a lie. "She's why I won't leave Earth."

I knew it. Anna's heart swells. *How could he...? He kissed me...*

James approaches Anna, wraps his arms around her, and says exactly what she needs to hear, "It's not like that."

Yeah right. It never is, is it? Anna's hands turn into fists and she leans them against his chest. *I could ... kill him.* She pushes him away. *Oh, God. Don't think it.*

He lets go. "She's the only one who can end this."

Anna steps back.

"My Dad," he says. "Mr. Pierson, was hired by a secret agency"—his eyes draw away—"Meadowlark. We were hired to build a backup."

"A backup for what?" asks Anna.

"A backup plan to abandon Earth. It's only a matter of time before every person on this planet is dead."

"I don't believe that ..."

"It doesn't matter what you believe." He huffs and sits down on the desk. "It's math."

"So where is she? Is this her office?"

He laughs. "No." He crumples a piece of paper into a ball and throws it at the dragonfly. "It's her sister's. I have no idea where she is."

"Well, what do you know?"

He pulls another piece of paper from the desk, begins to crinkle it, and then stops. His eyes grow large and a smirk pulls at the corners of his lips like a light bulb went off.

"What?" What the hell is he looking at?

He stands up and hurries out of the office, toward the front doors.

They slide open.

Anna runs after him.

He heads for the VW van out front. Spider Woman is already waiting for them, sitting behind it's steering wheel. Everyone seems to know where they are going, except Anna. She wants to know, but stopping to ask would be stupid. It doesn't matter. All that matters is they are still alive. She is still alive.

James slides open the back door and hops in, pulling it shut, forcing Anna to take shotgun.

A breeze from the South—from the trailer park—from home —pushes Anna into the vehicle.

James tosses up a green tee-shirt. It lands on Anna's arm. She holds it out. It is the same design she bought from the Country Fair. Its screen-printed design is a circle that curves up the middle, forming a tree in its center.

A laugh slips out. *Now the Universe is just fucking with me.*

"What?" asks James.

"Nothing." Anna slides the shirt over the hospital gown. It fits snugly, like it was his past girlfriend's. "Thanks."

Spider Woman leans on the steering wheel, attempting a better view of the sky.

"So where are we going?" Anna leans, trying to see what Spider Woman is looking at.

Something flies high above — it is an owl.

"I don't need to know," Spider Woman says, sitting back, and looking at the road before them.

The van rumbles into gear and sails down the driveway.

"I trust," she says.

Oh, God, we're going to die. "Trust who?"

"Myself," Spider Woman says.

What? "You trust yourself?"

"Why wouldn't I?" she says. "If I don't know who I am, how can anyone else?" She glances back up at the sky. "People are far too quick to decide who they want you to be." She glances in the rearview mirror at James. "If you ever want to have sex again…"

Excuse me. Heat rises to Anna's cheeks, blushing them.

"You're going to have to learn to trust yourself too." She glances at Anna. "Or you'll die in this world."

Anna doesn't turn around to study James' reaction. In the corner of her eye, she can see him squirm in the backseat. She sinks a little, hiding her head from his view, resting against the window, watching her bald reflection follow her over the smooth lines of the highway.

The landmarks and buildings hugging the curb became familiar. They head through town. The café is a block away. The street is quiet, dark. Small fires spit smoke into the low-lying air between buildings.

The van skids to a stop outside the café's large broken window.

Why are we here?

A red maple leaf is the only thing moving. It flaps, half-stuck to the brick. The café is wrecked, but there is no evidence of the zombie hoard.

James scoots to the edge of the backseat, popping his head between the women. "Ten minutes, tops."

"I don't understand. Why are we here?" asks Anna.

Spider Woman nods at a lamppost across the street.

The grey owl swoops out of the smoke and perches.

Spider Woman hops out and heads for the broken front door. James follows. She reaches in through the broken glass panel, unlocks the door, and pushes it open.

The bell. Anna jumps out of the van and attempts to grab her —the door—but it is too late.

It jingles.

Shit.

The street stays quiet. Nothing moves.

Spider Woman goes in. Pieces of glass crunch beneath her bare feet.

Anna follows second, letting James take the rear.

Pieces of glass stick to Anna's feet, clinking as she walks deeper into the café. Her eyes are glued to the dragonfly. She slides into the booth, examining it.

There is a noise—a low hum—coming from the backroom.

What the...? Anna tiptoes around the counter, not wanting to see Kelley's body, but it is gone. A trail of dark blood leads to the back prep area. *She's gone.* Chills creep up her spine like spiders. *Shit.* One of those things—those zombies—could be standing on the other side of the espresso machine.

She has nothing to defend herself if there is a zombie. She remembers that there is a frying pan hung on the other side of the wall, behind the espresso machine. Anna reaches around the machine to grab it.

It isn't there.

Damn it. She peeks around to make sure. A line of cakes spans the prep table. The back door to the building is wide open. The hum of an engine flows in. Her heart pounds. She forces her feet to the door.

Ms. Tumult's Mercedes idles in the loading area, spanning two parking spots.

Anna glances back at the cakes. The urge to call Ms. Tumult's name washes over Anna, but the idea of being ripped to pieces erases that.

Mist rises from the frozen cakes that have recently been taken out. Anna looks at the walk-in. She needs something to defend herself before trying the door. She thinks about everything Ms. Tumult has given her: a job, advice, extra pastries at the end of every shift. She had been a woman Anna could look up to. *Fuck it.* She jerks open the freezer.

Ms. Tumult's body falls into Anna's arms. She is freezing. She doesn't say anything, but her eyes move.

Anna drags her out and kicks the door closed.

The car engine rumbles and chugs louder outside the wide open back door.

Anna wraps her arms around Ms. Tumult, rubbing her hands down her arms to warm her.

Her teeth chatter.

"Shit." James steps into the back, looks at Ms. Tumult and the open door, then sprints out the backdoor.

Son of a bitch.

He left us. The engine dies. He comes back inside, pulling the door shut. "The oven. Turn the oven on and put her beside it. And a cup of … something hot."

Anna doesn't have to move. James does everything: starts the oven, puts on a pot of coffee. He doesn't know Ms. Tumult only drinks cappuccinos. Though it doesn't really matter.

Anna drags her to the oven. *God, the heat feels good.*

James pours a cup of coffee, offering it out to the store owner.

Ms. Tumult's arms shake as she reaches for it. Anna slides her fingers along Ms. Tumult's, steadying her grip, until her lips touch the porcelain. The warm glow of the oven stretches over Anna's arms, her hands.

Shit. She could change to … no … don't think it. She yanks her hands away, pressing her palms to the floor.

James grabs a second mug from the counter and hands it to Anna. "I don't drink coffee."

"I know," he says.

Her fingers slide around the porcelain, brushing his. She wants to feel the warmth of his skin against hers, but pulls away before she kills him.

He grins, offers a cup to Spider Woman, and disappears into the back again.

Spider Woman comes around the counter. Her long braid weighs the hospital gown down against her breast. "So this is where you're hiding."

Ms. Tumult's body quivers against Anna's.

"Have you found the clue yet?" Spider Woman sits down opposite her, leaning against the cabinets.

No. I haven't found anything except ... Ms. Tumult?

A smile broadens from Spider Woman's lips. She warms her hands by the stove. Her palms rub against each other. It takes Anna back 10 years.

Dad pleaded with Mom for weeks before she allowed him to take Anna camping. It was the only vacation she ever took. He came up with this week-long schedule of all the cool things we were going to do. It went nothing like she expected, like he planned. It was supposed to take 10 hours to get to Yosemite National Park. Instead it took three days. They made it halfway before his piece of shit car broke down.

Day one. They stayed in a hotel while the local guy toyed with the car. Anna stared at the peeling wallpaper, waiting for sleep to save her. Dad left her in the room once the moon came out, returning as the soft blue glow of morning began to peek between the blinds.

Two days later, they were at the park gates. Dad was throwing a tantrum about the admission price.

"What do you mean it costs money to get into the park?" he says.

"Sir, you can walk in for free." The zit-faced high school kid forced a smile, thinking that would ward off my Dad.

"Walk in from where?" Dad tittered, digging out a ratty leather wallet from his pocket. He pulled a $20 out. A crinkled photograph fell onto the seat.

Anna grabbed it and slid it beneath her leg.

He handed over the money and they were off, into the park. The road wound deeper into the valley, taking their breath away as it went.

They struggled with pitching a tent until it grew dark.

Dad started a campfire. Its warm glow danced around their site, reaching into the darkness beyond. Anna expected him to tell a story, sit with her for a while, pretend she was more than an obligation he had to fulfill. He grabbed a sleeping bag from the trunk and chucked it toward the tent, took a second one out and rolled it across the backseat. "Climb in."

"What about the tent?"

"I'll take the tent," he looked into the darkness surrounding them—the forest. "In case there are any bears."

Anna hopped into the back and huffed. She wanted to sleep beneath the stars, watch the moon dance around the earth.

He kissed the top of her head and shut the door.

She watched him sit by the fire, warming his hands in its glow, rubbing his palms together.

Yosemite, Anna remembers.

Spider Woman glances at her, slowly nodding.

They have their destination, but something tells Anna it will take longer than three days.

Metamorphosis

Night is fading. The oven glows like a beacon for the infected. Ms. Tumult ceased shivering and lay sleeping with her head on Anna's lap.

Spider Woman eases the oven closed and turns it off. Shadows fill their empty cups.

The sound of flapping wings falls from the sky and rests at the broken window. An owl screeches into the café.

Anna startles, jumping to her feet, knocking Ms. Tumult off her lap.

It is the same dark-grey owl. Its large eyes flash yellow. It screeches again.

James is in the backroom, dragging a huge bag of coffee beans toward the back door. He lets go and it spills across the floor. He runs out to us. "What the fuck?"

Spider Woman stands, helping Ms. Tumult up. It is time to load up Ms. Tumult's Mercedes. James' van has more room, but the Mercedes would get them to the park faster. Anna was sure James just wanted to drive the damn thing. Why not though? The buildings of their past are burning, smoke condenses in the air, and screams cut through it all. There is no reason not to do what they want.

The owl blinks and takes flight—disappearing as fast as it had come.

"I gotta pee," says Anna heading for the bathroom. Just the thought of taking a road trip makes her have to go. Any dude can pull over and piss off the side of the road. Being born with a vagina, Anna has to hold it until a rest stop or something. Stopping at any building would increase their chances of death.

"Make it quick." James' eyes leave Anna's, watching the storefront for movement.

Anna bites her lip. *I should tell him I have to shit. Yeah, because that idea is attractive.* If she only had to pee, she would leave the door open. She steps into the bathroom. The mirror captures the stranger she has become. She watches herself push the door closed, sinking from view onto the toilet.

James' footsteps move away, no doubt stocking the Mercedes with a few last items.

Anna clamps down on the toilet. It still hurts to have a bowel movement. Three years. Three years of bleeding. It started the year after her first period. It took her a whole other year before she had the guts to tell Mom and Jeremy. It had been so hard to tell them. Her period ran its seven-day course, but she was still bleeding. She wiped forward, risking a yeast infection. It wasn't coming from there, so she leaned and wiped her ass.

Jeremy had knocked on the door.

"I'll be out soon." Her palms were sweaty and her fingers shook. "Would you give me a minute?"

His voice muffled against the door. "Hurry up."

He was working the night shift back then. He had woken up around dinner time, and needed two cups of coffee to wake his ass up … no wonder he had to shit.

Anna slides the paper out from beneath her. It was bloody. She was fucking bleeding from her ass. She dropped the paper, flushed, and watched the blood sink down the toilet's dark hole.

Jeremy tapped on the door, saying something—something she couldn't register.

She pulled up her pants and managed to get to the sink. Somehow she turned on the water, running her hands in it, staring at herself in the mirror. But she didn't feel like she was there anymore. The clock was set. There was only so much time she had before they would force their chemicals and radiation upon her.

"Hey, kiddo?" Jeremy softly knocked. "You all right in there?"

She yanked the door open.

His face was still pressed against it, and he fell in a little, catching the threshold to prevent his fall. Instead of getting mad, like expected—like Dad would do—he jammed his sweaty hand through her hair and pushed past her into the bathroom.

She moved before the door hit her in the ass.

Mom was in the kitchen pouring a glass of wine. It was day five of her giving up beer—switching to a "healthy" way of killing herself. She coquettishly closed the bottle.

The memory disappears in the cold café bathroom.

Anna is alone. Her sweaty palms stick to a ball of toilet paper in her fist. She wipes, looking for the color. There is none, not a drop. She wipes again and again. The toilet paper is clean. *It's clean. How? The ... Bloodwort?*

James taps on the door. "Hey, we've gotta go."

Anna flushes, letting him know she has heard, then takes her time washing her hands, looking at the woman in the mirror, feeling her wings unfold.

BLEEDING

Anna opens the door, grabs James, and pulls him close, forcing her lips against his.

He reciprocates, sliding his fingers to her hips, pressing his body harder against hers. His hand slides over her hip and down her thigh. He bites her lip and backs away, digging his fingers into her thigh. He says, "I can't."

"Yes, you can," Anna says.

"You're too young."

Fuck that. I ... we could die any moment. And I'm too fucking young? "I don't want to die a virgin."

He tilts his head. "You're not a virgin."

"Fuck you." Anna pushes him away. It is true, Anna isn't a virgin, but her body burns to feel him. *I shouldn't have said that.* But she did, and it couldn't be changed. *How dare he say that to me—say I'm not a virgin?* She begins to walk away. *He thinks I'm some slut.* She glances back at him. Her body aches. *I don't care.* She takes off her shirt, walks back over to him, pressing her breasts up against the buttons of his shirt, and forces her lips against his.

His fingers move up her back.

There is no way she is taking her lips away from his. She pulls back enough to ease the kiss and then deepen it again. The blood in her veins beats faster—harder. He is going to give her what she wants. She pulls her lips from his, slowly.

"When you turn eighteen, okay?" he says.

Fuck that. She slides her hand down his pants and wraps her fingers around his junk.

He gasps and pulls his groan back, pulling away from her hand. He scolds, "Anna."

She doesn't need to be reprimanded in a fucking world with no laws. *Fuck you.* She pulls her hand from his pants and heads for the backdoor.

"Your shirt...," he says, tossing it over.

She catches it, locking eyes with him. "You either take me now, or never."

His chest rises with the next breath.

Anna starts thinking about all the reasons he doesn't want her. Age wouldn't stop him, not in this world. Is it the shaved hair, the patches of ripped scalp, the bruises, the way the dragonfly hovers on her flat chest?

He steps closer, pinning his eyes to the floor. His fingers slide along her cheek and brush her neck. A gentle pull toward him is all she needs to come closer. He pulls her to him and she allows it, stopping an inch short of his lips. His breath pushes warm air into her mouth. His hand finds the curve of her breast and his thumb slides over it. She wants to kiss him, but she has already demanded so much, it isn't fair to force him anymore. She closes her eyes. The pounding in her heart feels like a million butterflies. The warmth of his breath intensifies. She withholds her own breath, taking in every beat of his.

He kisses her.

A wave of pure contentment—excitement—floods her, then falls straight off the cliff, into regret. He hadn't wanted to kiss her. She pulls back and he pushes deeper into the kiss. She is forcing it—herself—onto him, and it feels terrible. She leans back even farther, taking a step backward.

Both his hands cup her face, steadying her for another kiss.

She turns her head, looking out the backdoor. "Don't." She looks back at him. "I'm sorry. I know you didn't want to … and I'm not—"

He kisses her, holding it, until he pulls back enough to whisper, "You're old enough."

She bursts with laughter.

His fingers release from her face and he smiles, huffing out his own laugh.

The hum of the Mercedes flows into the café. The horn blares.

James grabs her hand and they sprint through the prep area, out the back door.

A mob of people, thugs, are coming down the alley toward us. Four guys.

Shit.

They don't look infected, but they don't look friendly, either.

Spider Woman waves to her companions from behind the Mercedes driver's seat. Ms. Tumult is asleep in the seat beside her.

The mob grunts at the sight of them. Three of the four wear frat-sweatshirts. Blood stains their outfits. The odd one is in the lead. They all have weapons: a crowbar, baseball bat, kitchen knife, and some kind of metal car wrench.

Anna's heart jerks.

James sprints for the Mercedes, pulling Anna along. He yanks open the back passenger door and shoves Anna in.

The guy with the crowbar swings at James. He ducks. The crowbar shatters the open car-door window.

Spider Woman floors the vehicle into reverse. The door careens into the guys. Crowbar-dude falls to the ground. The front tire crushes him, just missing James. Kitchen-knife guy releases a cry of agony. Spider Woman shoves the car into drive, shooting it forward. The car bumps the kitchen-knife guy's hip, sending him spinning. James crawls to a stand.

No. We can't leave him. Anna can't leave him.

James is disappearing in the rear view.

No. "Stop!"

She won't.

The third guy carries a baseball bat. He swings at James and misses. He lets go of the bat and takes a swing at James with his fists, punching him to the ground.

No. "What are you doing? Stop!" Anna yells.

Spider Woman glances at the rearview mirror. "He has done everything he was meant to do."

Fuck that. Anna throws open the door and jumps out of the moving vehicle. Her shoulder careens into the asphalt. Pieces of skin scrape off onto the concrete as she rolls, stopping upon impact with the side of a brick building.

The tires screech to a halt.

Fuck. That hurt. She pushes up off the road.

The driver's door pops open and Spider Woman steps out. "What are you doing?"

"What is right." Anna stands and runs for him.

James' attacker grabs the fallen baseball bat and swings it down. James rolls enough to dodge it, and it pounds the ground beside his head. The wrench-guy is right there. He throws a punch at James' face. James catches the guy in his throat. The guy's face reddens like a cherry. James throws him off to the side. The baseball-bat guy swings, and the weapon wallops James' stomach.

Anna jumps on the asshole, knocking him to the ground. The bat falls from the guy's hand as the weight of her body slams into his. He swings at her. It happens too fast. She closes her eyes and waits for the blow to her temple, for the crushing of her skull, the blood to fill her brain-cavity.

Nothing happens.

She opens her eyes.

James has hold of the guy's hand and twists it until it pops.

The last guy, with the wrench, wants to cower and retreat, but in obligation, charges them. He clenches the wrench so hard, his knuckles turn white. He charges and plows into James.

Anna picks up the baseball bat and swings it down—closing her eyes—and swinging it down again. Wrench-guy starts screaming. Anna doesn't stop, she doesn't want to open her eyes.

James says something.

The bat comes down again.

"Anna," says James.

She lifts the bat again, catches herself to stop, and opens her eyes.

Swollen-tears slide from the guy's eyes. James lays beneath him. Shadows in the distance shift.

Shit.

The Mercedes is gone.

How could she? Part of Anna wants to run out onto the main street, search for the taillights and curse her. But the owl is back, sitting atop a lamppost down the alley.

Shadows shift in the shops below it.

James shoves the guy's body off of him and climbs to his feet, grabbing Anna's hand and tugging her back into the café.

Rain pelts the ground and fills the puddles.

Rain. Anna yanks her hand away from his.

As they cross through the threshold, she glances back. The men lay unmoving on the pavement. *What have I done?*

James reaches for her hand. She pulls back further, staring at their bodies.

Dark shadows, brain-dead college kids poured down the alleyway.

James grabs her arm, pulling her into the prep area, flinging her in front of himself. "Go."

She sprints through the backroom.

James follows.

Echoes of zombie-moans follow them. They move too fast. James scoops a cake off the table and throws it at the closest one. The guy falls.

James yells at Anna, "Go, go!"

She rounds the counter and stops. The glow of the streetlight, reaches in for the mosaic dragonfly. *Take it.*

James bumps into her.

She hops onto the bench and grabs hold of it.

"What are you doing?" he yells.

Another zombie rounds the espresso machine. He is leaner, faster.

Anna tugs on the dragonfly. Goddamn thing wouldn't budge.

James doesn't ask any more questions. He hops on the booth, reaches around her, and yanks the damn thing off the wall.

The zombie grabs James' leg.

James whacks him with the dragonfly. Pieces of mirror rain to the floor. James grunts, pushing the guy back—until he falls over. James hops down, stomping the guy's face until he stops moving. He grabs Anna's hand, pulls her out of the booth, and sprints for the front door—the van on the curb outside.

The owl swoops down, landing in the window, screeching at them.

Anna pulls back a little and James jerks her forward.

The owl leans in, fluffs its wings and screeches louder.

Shadows move in the broken doors and windows across the street.

Anna and James clear the front door. He propels her toward the passenger side door of the van. She careens into it.

"Sorry," he says, running around to the driver's seat. He slides in and chucks the dragonfly into the back.

Anna hops in.

The zombie mob piles down the alleyway behind them, focused on the café's back door. A few faces turn their attention their way.

"Go," says Anna.

They start for the van.

James twists the key in the ignition and the van sputters. "Shit."

No.

He forces it again and the engine rumbles a second longer than before, then craps out.

Anna slumps in the passenger seat and glances at the side view mirror. A zombie is two feet away. His eyes connect with hers in the mirror. *Shit.* It throws its fist into the window. Glass rains into the wounds of Anna's scalp.

The van rumbles and shoots forward.

The zombie's arm catches between the door and the mirror. The smell of death seeps in with the air, dragging the corpse along. Anna pushes herself to sit up. Fragments of glass cut into her skin. *Fuck.* She sits back.

The zombie swings its free hand into the van.

Anna swings, attempting to punch the asshole in it's face, but pieces of glass dig deeper into her skin as she clenches her fists. She closes her eyes and concentrates on the shards of glass, the small threads slicing deeper into her skin. *Water.* They melt into drops of water.

The zombie swings again and it's fingers slide over Anna's shaved head, grabbing hold of her sleeve.

She knocks the zombie away, and it falls off. Its body rolls and sinks along the highway, disappearing behind them.

"You okay?" James grips the steering wheel tighter, glancing down at Anna's hands.

"Yeah," she says. "It's just a few scratches."

"Jesus, Anna," he says, looking at her forehead. "That one looks bad."

She slides ass through the sandpaper of glass covering the seat, and pulls down the small sun-visor. Its mirror shows her the inch-long piece of glass sticking out sideways from her scalp. The flesh throbs around it. A thin line of blood pools at its edge. Anna pinches the flat sides of it, envisioning what the molecular structure could be.

"Don't," James says. "If it's deep … if you pull it, it could be keeping you from bleeding out."

"Bleeding out?"

"Yeah." He sits up and hunches farther over the steering wheel, pressing his eyes closer to the windshield. "I'll pull over in about five minutes. We should clear town first."

The wound throbs and burns. The sliced-tissue pulsates against the smooth surface of Anna's skin. *When? When are we going to stop so I can get this…* Her stomach pits. *Get this shit out of me?* She leans her head against the window, watching the road blur.

Mom's smiling face floats into her thoughts. She was so nervous the first time she brought Jeremy home to meet Anna. It wasn't long after she broke up with Kevin. The aqua paint of her bedroom walls—the color of the bar's door—fills the memory with a cold comfort—comfort Anna needs in that moment. It is so cold. The sound of the air rushing by, pushing into the cracks of the van, deepens the chill.

James rests his hand on Anna's thigh. "We're almost there."

Five minutes is so long—too long.

Anna glances up at the mirror, tilting her head to see the big fucking piece of glass. Stomach acid leaches up her throat, forcing her to retch. She presses her fingers to her lips, restraining to vomit.

DITCH

JAMES PULLS OVER TO THE SIDE OF THE ROAD. THE Volkswagen van headlights illuminate the long grass stretching for miles all around. He climbs into the back, digging through surfer gear, blankets, and granola bars.

Anna stares at the beams of light capturing the five feet of the dark road before them—her path. The wound throbs. Acid churns in her empty stomach. The air grows thick with fog, heavy to inhale. Her lungs burn as she restrains each breath longer, trying to ease the pounding in her head.

"Okay," he says.

Anna looks at the shard of glass and squeezes it. *I can do this*. She concentrates on the glass.

A centimeter melts into water, but the glass slides deeper through the tissue.

"Shit." Anna panics.

"What?" James leans past her, opening the glove box, and pulls a small metal first-aid kit out. The damn thing looks like it is from the 1950s. Anna places a bet that the Band-Aids aren't even sticky. He opens back its rusted latch. Inside is a sandy piece of surfer's wax, and those crusty, yellowish Band-Aids. He pushes the wax aside and pulls out a sewing needle.

Only a guy would keep a bar of wax in his first aid kit. Anna laughs, washing away the pain for a second.

"It's the block of wax," he says, "isn't it?"

Anna lets her lips fade back to normal. Smiles will prove to be hard to come by. She means to savor each one. *I can do this*. She looks back at the mirror and narrows her eyes on the piece of glass. She sticks her finger against it, melting it a little more. Diluted blood overflows the cut. She pulls her finger out.

James' eyes widen and he leans back a little. "What are you doing?"

"I ... I can't..." I can't change—it into water.

"You have to," his voice softens.

She looks away from the mirror, at the headlights—the pathetic illumination of her fucking life—the path she is supposed to follow—the darkness trying to get in, to leave her suffocating. She glances back at the mirror.

An ambulance and it's flashing red lights break up the dark city behind us. There is no siren. It's spiraling red beams cut through the soft yellow glow.

James moves into the middle of the road.

"What are you doing?" Anna yells.

"Getting us some help," he says.

"What do you mean? They're going to run your ass over."

The red, spinning lights come quick. Their beams cut across James' chest.

He holds his hands up in a plea to stop.

It gets closer. Anna can see the driver's face—a young kid, her age, scared as shit. The vehicle sways a little. His lips sync the word, "Move."

"Move!" Anna yells.

James lowers his hands and dives into the ditch across the road.

The ambulance swipes the driver's side-door, taking off the side mirror. The van rocks.

Oh, my God. Is he dead? He's dead. He's dead. Shit. Nothing moves in the ditch. *Shit.* Anna jumps out of the van and sprints across the road. *Shit.* Cold air scrapes at her body. "James?"

He doesn't say anything.

Where the fuck is he? It is too dark. Everything is dark. Nothing moves. Anna screams, "James?"

He moans.

Where? Left? Right? She can't see anything.

He moans again.

Left. She turns, takes one step, and falls on top of him.

He grunts. "You found me."

She had found him, in the most unpredictable way.

DREAM

THE AMBULANCE'S LIGHT DIES IN THE DISTANCE.

"Well." James digs his hands into the moist earth and sits up, flinging globs of soil off, before wiping them on the clean spots of his pants. "That guy needs his certification revoked."

Anna can't believe it—that is all he has to say. A breeze crosses her lips and a smile follows.

He reaches for Anna's hand, interlacing his fingers with hers. She pulls away. "No ... I'll ..."

He tightens his grip, pulling her close. Her chest presses up against his side. He moans with pain. His free hand brushes her cheek and pulls her lips to his. "You ready to grow up?"

She bites her lip and goes for another kiss. *I'll turn him to ….* *I could never forgive myself if … Fuck.* The idea of killing him eats Anna up. She pulls away, wrapping an arm around his torso instead.

He moans as she helps him stand up. They climb out of the ditch. Anna looks twice before crossing the dark, desolate road.

Wind blows in from the West, scuffing at the wounds of Anna's scalp.

James climbs into the back of the van, reaching for Anna's hand—knowing full well she could kill him at any moment with a single touch.

She slides her fingers between his and allows him to carry her off, to save her from the encompassing darkness. Once the door is shut, he lets go.

Anna returns to the passenger seat and stares at the sun-visor mirror.

James takes the driver's seat, pulls a liquor bottle out from beneath it, and unscrews its top. Everclear is some nasty shit. It burns when swallowed and leaves a girl completely vulnerable to whatever company she keeps. He leans closer and pours it into the cut.

It burns. *Fuck.* Anna leans away from him. "What the fuck, man?"

"Sorry," he says. "You don't want it all to get infected."

"Why not? Can't I disintegrate that too?"

He looks away.

"What?"

"No," he says. "Not unless you have a teacher?"

"Like a monk or something?"

"Like Ms. Murphy."

Shit.

"You can't risk getting infected." He leans closer. "Put out your hands."

She does so, and he pours the alcohol slowly over them. *What a waste.*

He closes the bottle and moves into the back as Anna returns her attention to the mirror.

The cut is swollen. It throbs. Her stomach roils and she shoves her finger down into the warm, wet flesh until its tip cuts against the glass. There isn't much glass left inside the wound. She concentrates and nothing happens. "It's not working."

"Harder," James says.

She closes her eyes and presses her finger deeper. The glass slices through her fingerprint and pops. Relief eases the acid churning in her stomach. She fully exhales before withdrawing her finger. It is covered in blood and the fresh cut on her fingertip oozes with crimson liquid.

James kneels beside her, presses a hand against her head, and digs the sewing needle into the swollen flesh.

Euphoria pulses through her veins and blurs the reflection in the mirror. The alcohol penetrated her body from the wound.

"There," he says, pulling back, wiping Anna's blood off his hands, onto his pant leg. He grabs the bottle of liquor, opens it, and pours the liquid over the wound, then passes the bottle to her.

They should save it in case anything else went wrong, but Anna needs it to dull the stress pulsating through her veins. The liquid burns down her throat with one gulp, sinking into her bloodstream. She offers it to James.

He shakes his head, declining.

Anna needs it more than him, but he looks like hell and she has had enough. She offers it again.

He takes it, bowing his head. After a few swigs, he climbs into the back and lays down, folding his hands behind his head, gazing up.

They are safe. She lays beside him and he nuzzles closer, letting his body radiate warmth for her.

The moon peeks out, guiding them to dream.

GONE

SLEEP BRINGS RELIEF, BUT NOTHING GOOD ENOUGH TO hold onto.

Anna's head is killing her. The cut throbs and the Everclear leaves an unwelcome headache.

James is gone.

Anna sits up, searching left and right. The blue window curtains are drawn open, but there is no sign of him outside.

The city of Corvallis burns behind them.

The side door opens and James gets in.

Rain splatters against the windows and begins to pound on the roof.

"Morning. Hell of a headache, huh?" he says.

Relief floods her, pushing her back down, giving her heart a chance to stabilize.

He grabs the first-aid kit and sets it outside, collecting rainwater. Worry fills his face and is evident with the slow slide of his hand over his forehead. "Maybe we should go back."

Anna looks back at the dark plumes of smoke rising from the city.

"You're ... I shouldn't have kept you here," he says. "I can —"

"No." Anna knows what he is going to say. He can send her up there—into space. "I'm staying here," she says. She looks out the door, to an open field. She can almost see the buttercups that reflect the sun's rays in the summer. She looks at James, but his eyes are on the field.

He looks at her—the Earth—in a way Anna has never seen before. A lump forms in his throat.

"I'm not supposed to leave," Anna whispers.

He nods, leans against the wall of the van, and motions her over. She nuzzles in beside him, resting her hand on his stomach. He cringes with pain. She leans away, unbuttoning the top of his shirt. Button by button, his breath deepens. His shirt falls open. *Damn.* His flat stomach is ripped with muscles, but a dark bruise takes up the entirety of his side.

The sound of an engine approaches from town. Anna leans back enough to see between the back curtains.

It is a Hummer.

Shit.

"What?" James tries to sit up, but only makes it halfway.

"It's them," she says.

His eyes meet hers. "Maybe if... Lock the doors. Pull the curtains, but do it slow."

Anna does as he says and slides back down beside him on the floor.

He wraps his arm around her, pulling her tight against his side.

The Hummer rolls to a stop outside the van. They weren't lucky enough for the agents to have kept going. Their doors creak open and slam shut.

James slides his free hand across Anna's cheek, nudging her chin—her lips—to his. He presses them harder against hers, sinking into it as he exhales, wrapping his arm a little tighter.

An agent tugs on the driver's side door. It is locked.

The second agent says, "Break the fucking thing."

What do we do? Anna should pull away from James and panic, but it doesn't matter anymore. All they have is this moment. Anna knows it is going to be their last. From here on out, it is all going to change. She knew it when the old Native appeared in the café. She knew things would be different.

The driver's side window shatters. An agent pops his head in. "Hey! You two. What the fuck are you doing?"

In reflex Anna begins to turn her head away from James, to face the man, but James forces another kiss onto her.

"I asked you a question," the guy yells.

The other agent rounds the van and smashes in the side door window.

James pulls his lips away, leaning his forehead against Anna's. "Go."

"What?" *I'm not leaving you.*

"Open this door." The agent tugs on the side door.

Anna begins to turn that way, but James refocuses her back to his eyes. "You've got to get away." He nods once. "Do you understand?"

"But—"

"No." He grabs onto her arms. His voice softens a little and his grip eases, "No."

The guy outside shoots the door handle and yanks it open.

James lets go.

Rear Views

Everything happens so fast. The agent punches James in the mouth, yanks him out the door, and throws him to the ground. The second agent approaches around the back with a baton and whacks James in the side.

James lifts his head. Blood spits from his lips as he screams at Anna, "Go!"

Her heart jerks. She jumps up from her spot, whacking her head against the ceiling.

The first agent looks at Anna as his partner whales against James again.

Anna hops into the driver's seat, scoots out the door, and sprints for the Hummer.

The agent yells, "Hey!"

Shit. I can't make it. He's going to get me—beat the shit out of me. Her toes dig into the asphalt, tearing the skin. She doesn't look back for fear of falling, slowing. She knows he is coming fast and it won't be as simple as opening the door and hopping in to escape. He will expect that. She takes a hard left and starts down the road. He'll either stop or follow. *Shit.* She has to look back. If she doesn't, she will have no way to know where he is. *Fuck this.* She pivots all her weight to turn back, and runs at the fucker. Sure enough he is in hot pursuit and all she has to do is clothesline him. Anna flings out her arm, catching him with it, and knocking him to the ground.

The air expels from his lungs as he falls to the asphalt. His head hits the road—hard. He moans.

Anna screeches to a halt and goes back, yanking the samurai sword from his holster.

His eyes roll to the back of his head.

She jams the blade into his stomach.

He reaches for the sword, grabbing its blade as it slices through his fingers.

Oh, my God. Anna lets go of it, steps back—away. She can't really be here, couldn't have done that. *How could I? It's only a movie. This isn't real.* She spins around, looking back at the van.

James lay on the ground, bloody. His assailant has stopped pulverizing him, noticing his partner's lifeless body beneath Anna, and he charges her.

The Hummer is six feet away. Anna rips the sword out of the guy and runs for it. The door is unlocked and she jumps in behind the wheel, feeling for the keys. They are in the ignition, just waiting for her.

The agent is a few feet away from Anna.

James has climbed to hands and knees.

I can't leave him.

The agent draws a gun, aiming it at the passenger window.

Anna punches the Hummer into drive.

The agent takes the shot.

The rear passenger window shatters.

He takes another.

The bullet shoots through the back window and exits through the front, just below the rearview mirror.

Anna swerves, creating a harder target.

Another shot pierces the passenger headrest. A fourth tears apart the side view mirror. Three more bullets shatter the asphalt before the agent dwindles in the rearview mirror.

Anna jams the gas pedal down to the floor, holding it there. The empty grass-seed fields blur by. It is miles by the time she can ease off the gas pedal.

The speed gauge levels and she sinks back into the seat. *I shouldn't have left him.*

The fields drain their color as the clouds take over.

She can still go back. But if he isn't already dead, the agent would surely enough have killed him—and her.

She isn't ready to die. Her stomach knots and nausea builds in her stomach.

Up in the distance is an apple orchard and a long driveway, leading to what is sure to be a house.

Anna pulls off to the side of the road, well before the driveway, hidden by the tree's sagging branches. A four-foot high, barbed-wire fence hugs the property. She throws open the car door, takes its keys, and kicks down one of the flimsy fenceposts, trespassing into the shelter of apple trees. A few leaves hang in autumn colors above her. She paces, wanting so badly to go back and rescue James. She reaches for an apple and it bursts into water droplets.

A dog barks in the distance behind her.

She touches another and it falls like a cup of water into her hand. She flops down to the ground. It is no use. She grabs a handful of fallen leaves and drops them into the wind, letting them drift further away.

Screams erupt from the farm house far down the driveway. It is time to move on. Anna stands, runs her fingers over the bare ness of her head and reaches for an apple again. She digs her feet into the ground, grounding with the earth, connecting with its electrical field, and twists the apple from the tree. She takes a bite out of it and, for a moment, believes she may have a chance in this world of death.

The screams come again, closer, and Anna leaves the orchard for the road again. She hops into the driver's seat.

A tiny spider drops down from behind the rearview mirror, spinning on a single thread of web.

Anna looks into the mirror, gazing on the path back to town —back home. She has made it out of the trailer park and all she wants is to go back home.

ACKNOWLEDGEMENTS

To my readers, for demanding that I continue the story. To my three amazing children, for reminding me to dream, and always showing me the beauty in this world. To Sarah for teatime and all the sanity it brings. To Lisa W., Lisa B., Kari, and Suzanne, for reading this first and making it better. To my first editor, Cheryl, for squeezing in my projects. To Partners in Crime Book Service for an amazing edit on the second edition. To my writers group: Bill, Carla, Diana, Charlie, James, and Suzanne, for graciously reading first drafts. To Joanna, Sarah, and Suzi, for kick'n it at weekly writing sessions that always motivated and distracted.

To those who live in poverty.
May you realize that we all look at the same moon.

ABOUT THE AUTHOR

Julie Embers graduated from Stockton University with a degree in Biology. Writing ignited her journey into enlightenment. In a constantly changing world, she writes full-time . She recently traded the Pacific Northwest for the Gulf beaches of Florida with her kids and french bulldog.

WWW.JULIEEMBERS.COM

www.ingramcontent.com/pod-product-compliance
Lightning Source LLC
Chambersburg PA
CBHW030104260626
47156CB00008B/2514